THE COTTON BREATH

ROBIN THRONE

ANAPHORA LITERARY PRESS

QUANAH, TEXAS

ANAPHORA LITERARY PRESS
1108 W 3rd Street
Quanah, TX 79252
https://anaphoraliterary.com

Cover design by Rivertown Creative
Interior design by Anna Faktorovich, Ph.D.

Printed in the United States of America, United Kingdom and in Australia on acid-free paper.

Prologue appeared previously as "The Cotton Breath" in *Crab Fat Magazine*

Simon's segment appeared previously as "Run North" in *Trampset*

Cover image: Sea island cotton plant, *Gossypium barbadense*. Botanical illustration from *Koehler's Medicinal Plants*, edited by Gustav Pabst, Koehler, Germany, 1887.

Published in 2019 by Anaphora Literary Press

The Cotton Breath
Robin Throne—1st edition.

Library of Congress Control Number: 2018951384

Library Cataloging Information
Throne, Robin, 1960-, author.
    The cotton breath / Robin Throne
    152 p. ; 9 in.
    ISBN 978-1-68114-463-4 (softcover : alk. paper)
    ISBN 978-1-68114-464-1 (hardcover : alk. paper)
    ISBN 978-1-68114-465-8 (e-book)
1. Fiction—Literary. 2. Fiction—Romance—Historical—American.
3. Fiction—African American—Historical.
PN3311-3503: Literature: Prose fiction
813: American fiction in English

THE COTTON BREATH

ROBIN THRONE

partus sequitur ventrem

"*that which is brought forth follows the womb*"

—*Roman civil law*

PROLOGUE

B y 1920, Martha's brothers had long since sold the last crop of Sea Island cotton, and some loyal civil servant had failed to save the seeds of the most precious gold ever seen in the Sea Islands. The inland-grown plant was no match for what had been on water, and weevil came and brought a smothering death to the long, silky fiber that had clothed the queen and made Martha's own nightshirts.

The brothers left then, off to find their own cotton in whatever better form it took, but she could never leave the island parcel. *It was her temporary home, she was just a tenant,* she would say, but it was really because she just had too much of Cypress in her. They had all told her so when they'd left, hats in hand, fear of the unknown pumping up their blood and visions beyond for better, dry ground—landlocked— laughing at the mockery of words that did not fit.

They had run north till they found work-for-hire that lasted more than a week and dug in to blend with a place for once not named for captains, planters, and their heredities or even old trails of false cotton hope. There were no reminders of those acres given and taken back, begged and procured, then taken again. They bought their plats with clean titles and kept them till they were dead, buried, and had cleanly passed them on to heirs who had no idea of the true value of such gifts. Those boys knew what it meant to see a singular deed, but it was together that they burned their mortgages. Only they could understand the sentiment of their solemn fire-centered ceremonies, the way they reminded them of the burnings from before, hidden away in that boarded-up place on the inside, soaked by old gin and deep self-laceration that cut faint, pallid ghosts, now not even heard or fully remembered.

Yet there, always there. That old South would not be revisited in the sober, waking hours, discontent and dormant only until the day when all hell broke loose and the spirit of the grandmothers wrested free of the edge water—as ol Conjur had predicted—and hovered high to feed them all. Sea Island cotton would never return like in the old days, for something so precious can now only be dreamed of, dreamed of like that first breath of freedom that comes just before you think it's your last.

CONTENTS

BEFORE

Ol Conjur knew well enough he could steal precious early morning time at the waterside, long before Master Planter ever awoke, as long it was early, still dark, and no sun globe was inching its head above the sea line. That morning he sensed the coming in his bones as strongly as he had the storm in '59, when he had forewarned Master Planter and the Master, in turn, his planter cousins. The families had fled from that hurricane to their inland Savannah or Beaufort summer homes, but this time there would be no warning. This one he would keep to himself while he viewed the level horizon, invaded by the vertical masts erect against a plum dawn.

Today the gales would bring an influx of the bluest blue.

Bluer than water.

Bluer than sky.

Bluer than that yellow child for whom she had saved herself last night from this blue-black life by never declaring its beller.

Born blue.

By midnight, black.

This blue would not be for keeping restless haints at bay.

This blue would be for protecting on the inside.

This blue would be the one for which they had all been waiting.

Ol Conjur was so thankful that morning, he slapped his knee and jimmied his nose up to his eyes in a tight squint.

So very tired, but perhaps some sleep could finally come for all of them now.

Blues here at last.

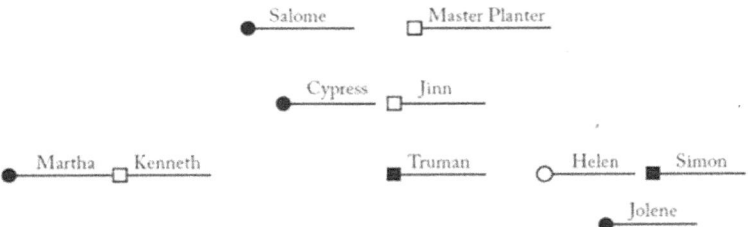

For at least 300 years, the lone, ancient cypress had guarded the marsh side of Tabby Place, and more than one old soul had gone to this tree called holy and planted offerings at its base, the place where its spirit met the ground, seeking out answers from this place.

The triangular bare and knobby roots were the reminder of the seamless skims between sea and sky, earth and water, growth and life. Each means, in its own incantation from the heavens, was another's gold, and each momma's son saw them leveled across the backs of those in servitude to a master.

Indigo.

Rice.

Cotton.

The cypress had seen the first of the Captain's family arrive by ship and place their goods at its base like the old superstitions advised, saw them set their sights on the clearing beyond for building a settlement. Perhaps another tribe had cleared it in readiness for something else, but the Captain's family cared not.

Growth.

This was to be their kingdom now.

Indigo.

Rice.

They had traveled far, and this was to be home—in a new land accessible only by waterways, their own familiar. They had lived on water long enough, and it was now time to put down dry and rest.

This respite was going to be quite a long one for the women, but the men were soon called back by the waves and work and a human harvest much more lucrative than any on land.

They began to fill up their ships with bodies stacked like their children's chessmen, neatly stowed in a board case.

Up and down.

Lateral.

Hooked ankle-to-wrist like inanimate rooks and knights till they bled and festered. Not ebony or ivory. Bona fide murky bodies with blood and guts after all.

The island routes boomed as more royalists found their way to where rice and indigo could be harvested by hand—dark, experienced hands from directly due east that through sheer will survived the Middle Passage and with good odds were placed outside the poison row; hands that already knew the ways of water, marsh, sand, and tide;

hands that captured growth cycles as second nature.

They and their children's children would harvest the others' gold for decades to come.

Unfortunately, the owners did not view it as the tree of death that it always had been, and death would soon find them. But coin has ever blurred many an ending, even today.

So yes, they found their fortunes here, but some of them—those not so bent for sail—eventually claimed the land for dirt and plantings that were desired abroad. But where the land's real money lay would always be in the quest for the real gold.

And gold they would find in these plantings and exports beyond their wildest envisioning.

Halfwit farmers, their sea-loving cousins called them behind their backs when far off at sea again and well out of earshot. But they did become the wealthiest of proprietors and no longer dirtied their hands with deals that made their skin crawl.

Those deals would take years to shed, however.

In the meantime, the farmers would outfit the captives with warmth and food and protection from their own naïveté. They would pick their favorites and leave the rest to be taken by the sailors or sold to those less fussy about muscle tone, full bites, abrasions, and hunger-lined rib cages.

Malnourishment could be corrected more easily than resistance, and the early island planters had no time for domestication.

Cotton.

Cotton was to become the grandest kingdom of all.

So the early island farmers took the best of the captives, the calm and quiet and the ones who would bring Tabby Place up to its glory days, which of course only lasted until the Captain's card lust turned it over in a badly-dealt hand to Master Planter, who passed it on to Junior, the only Master Planter known to Salome's line.

Yes, it was Master Planter who would be at the helm until the day Cypress came, and at long last, change would fall on them all.

FORCED PARTITION SALE

PARTITION AUCTION NOTICE

The County of Beaufort in the state of South Carolina will auction the following said property at **121 N Blackgum Tree Road** in a partition by sale. Please note: auction will take place **July 31, 1973**.

Any residents of the estate must vacate the premises by the date of the recorded deed of sale. Departure (and removal of all personal belongings) must be executed in a timely and peaceable manner. If residents fail to vacate and yield possession of the property, legal proceedings will be instituted to obtain possession of the property and estate. Such proceedings may result in a criminal indictment on unyielding residents and subsequent attorney fees or court costs as sanctioned under county law; furthermore, the owner of the property and estate may bear additional punitive charges in accordance with South Carolina legislation against the unlawful detention of state property and refusal to comply with county injunctions.
This Notice does not relieve residents of payments or financial obligations to the estate, such as property taxes and/or fees owed (etc.) prior to the date of its sale.

Sea Island
Sea Island Parish
Beaufort County, South Carolina

There it was—tacked on the cracked, taped glass of a long-ago-sprung aluminum door, the one on North Blackgum Tree Road that on a peculiarly wintry spring day had brought Martha to her knees and the blackberries to the ground.

It was quite strange to fixate on such exterior details as the already useless cellophane tape, pulled away from the edges of the door and of harsh words. It was like the torn soul of a bullied child, head lowered under the onslaught of name-calling, shying from the incessantly ripping taunts. There was no escape from disparagement in either case.

And the tacked words might've just broken away on their own accord to escape the present reality. The trouble later would be in trying to relocate those words to make meaning of that horrid circumstance. So insecure was the fixture of notice that it seemed it might at any moment lift itself off the ill-fitting crooked-framed door and take flight—flying away fast and furious from events both bygone and soon-to-be-faced, just as so many others had already done.

The bottom corner of the notice had begun to slip through its cheap plastic sleeve as if slipping from some sort of shield that would have kept it in place against a natural marsh neighbor. What was to be known would be known by court summons, and in some ways, it was a fate no one was going to be able to stop now.

All Martha had then were the logical sensibilities Cypress had instilled in her and an unwavering belief in the security of cold hard facts and figures. Her appreciation for the certainty Cypress had always practiced and expected steeled Martha in the thickness of uncertainty called by a recurrent situation. She loved the certainty of the crises her mother had always expected, even with the uncertain aspects of this consecutive calling.

Her turn now.

Ø

There was one glaring stain on the Developer's otherwise perfect plan in 1959, one visual blight amidst his modern and sleek plantation design.

It was not the remnants of the tabby structures of the old plantation house and its outbuildings. The Developer had already offered up those ruins to the state, remnants of a war and lifestyle that would not be forgotten in his era.

It was not the Developer's sensibility.

He was the wizard of a lifestyle that was fit for the elite.

Better than. More than.

Conjured it up in his own mind and made it so.

So pleased with himself, he was.

What bothered him, the stain on his vision, was the 48-acre fringe jumble of a 300 square foot tabby base without a building onset, a shabby old barn, and an unsightly aluminum-wood conglomeration that his designer would not even consider for retention. They joked of it often. "The *new* aluminum model home." They'd laughed a good one over that image.

Shuddered, really.

It all had to go.

More so, it had to be taken up.

Find an heir, he'd said to his attorneys even then.

Let's buy this one out.

∅

Cypress had raised three fatherless children on some 40 tillable she had inherited from Salome—lost, earned back twice, paid for once—and Cypress would writhe in her grave for eternity, Martha knew full well, if she was the one who gave in now.

JINN

Control the seed.
Control the money.
Master Planter's philosophy had always been quite simple but became increasingly difficult before the Blues arrived. In the years since acquiring Tabby Place from the Captain, he had found Jinn, and, of course, that was what had fueled those most prosperous of years.

Planter diligently filed the patents to protect his work until the extra-long staple was perfected and then received the news the capitol patent office had burned. Fortunately, his records had been meticulous, and he'd re-filed again and again for the next twenty years. It was only after those record-shattering first bales had first left Savannah for Liverpool that he knew that a second, more lucrative revenue stream would begin, and subsequently, the bale stamp would become more conspicuous for those who followed the money.

By 1850, his 150 bales had sold for a record average 60 cents per pound, double that of his two prior decades of effort, and he became known from Charleston to the St. Mary's River as sheer cotton genius.

His dollar-pound bales were legendary, if not mythic, and no one but the English and Planter first knew of these trades. No other island plantation attained such prices and most others topped out at 50 cents a pound. The year before the Blues arrived, twenty others had finally given in to purchase his seed, after learning his seed sharing was internal diversion, and Master Planter, the most celebrated among them, had led their celebrations and secessionist declaratives of independence to shed the cumulative taxes sent north. After all, the wealth should not leave the state. Why should it feed the northern bureaucrats and their mounting munitions? Everyone knew by then whose taxes could and would be paid.

Sadly, Master Planter could never acquire enough land and money to alleviate his ultimate fear of exposure. He had fallen into that false belief that has plagued many a good man that the price per pound was a measure of his personal invincibility, his own worth, which any mature soul knows was bound to ebb and recede like the tide. High tide would certainly not last, but he had no debt and was so flush with cash he began to build and to please Missus Planter beyond her dreams with updates and lavishness to Tabby Place that she had begged for throughout the Forties and had finally realized her envisioned mansion.

The double portico with dual-veranda could be seen by every steamer cruising enroute from Sea Island to Charleston, and the mounting cash reserves were also quickly absorbed by a complete renovation of their inland summer home, a refurbished federal style fueled by fresh cotton wealth that finally gave her the curved teak staircase and T-shaped floor plan that offered the best ventilation possible for the hottest months.

Early on, Missus Planter had firmly decided to consult the designer of the federal buildings and to learn from them. She would not waste time admiring Charleston Spanish style or Savannah's Georgian or Greek revivals. Let her tasteless island cousins follow that suit; she was now a secure cotton queen who would set the trends for her neighbors and extended family follow.

Yet when Master Planter decided to expand the kitchen quarters beyond the under-rooms nestled next to the kitchen and build an unheard-of set of separate cabins for Salome and ol Granny, Missus Planter turned the lumber deliveries away from her great portico, and the sound of her shrill note cast a wide and deep fear among the kitchen women. However, Master Planter had many tools to placate his sharp-tongued wife and soothed her with textiles and even a visit from Evan St. Clair, a Boston jeweler who set his mother's English gems into contemporary settings that Missus Planter would claim later—after the secession convention—that she had designed herself.

As Master Planter had predicted, she soon turned away from his comforts for the house girls and set her sights instead on European furniture and fashion, globes and rich carpets, spending more and more time on emergency retail trips to Paris and the orders arriving weekly from the West Indies. The time—oh the time—sped so fast as she worked to oversee these shipments back to the island and then inland of the splendor she had procured. Treasures only she had the refined taste to select in person—she spent weeks at a time doing so, and neglected Master Planter, who spent most of his hours at the seed bench alongside Jinn anyway.

He might as well have been one of them.

Missus Planter thought her evil thought and then brushed it swiftly from her mind as if she had not thought it. She would not pay for his
deeds. *It was no wonder he took up his sundry pleasures,* she convinced
herself. *He needed something to comfort those old bones beyond the west
wicket,* she decided. Keep it at bay, beyond her house, and she had less
to dirty her own thoughts and membranes. *Let him pay in final judg-
ment and let us then see who is pure and right in the hereafter.*

Near the end, it was these righteous thoughts that kept her buy-
ing and spending cotton currency, the CC she floated as if it were real
monetary note among her retailers with no regret, as Master slept now,
more often than not, like a soldier at the outpost, and not between the
silky cotton sheets spun of his own best fiber.

All for the good of the family and the CC mansions!

This was precisely the thought that allowed her to close her eyes
at night, rid of the tossing and turning that was her husband's nightly
curse.

Control the seed.
Control the money.

This took them both to accomplish.

∅

Cypress was more than the land; she was the ocean that bounded Sea Island.

Even when alive, she had been deep and wide and unseen.

Like a sea of her own making.

Still alive somehow in her death, she held mysteries that only came clear with time, made lucid to the generations of each new day.

Young to old—old to young.

Timeless and unfathomable.

Cypress had endured even when her children could not. She had returned even when the afterlife could not sustain her mother and Jinn.

She had never really departed, only in flesh. Cypress was stronger than all of them, even abiding death, and her spirit had persisted to prove it.

Her spirit always was.

Always is.

Cypress had whispered to her children, and some believed her, remembered she would never leave them. Others forgot.

Or those children had never actually believed, merely put on that they did.

Below the crimson horizon where sand met sky, somewhere off in that deep cavern in which the unknown lived among the vast waves penetrable only at sunset, lay her greatest gifts.

Gifts of purpose.

Responsibilities of birth.

Only the most ardent of spirits ever sought out Cypress to fetch her memories, bring them into the light of a new morning.

Back when Cypress was alive, she had never ventured far from shore. This remained true—even after the death of her body—Martha was sure because of her sleep visitations, which now occurred almost nightly.

As the Blues had come, so did Cypress return, and in her fiercest presence yet.

This was how Martha got the signal that it was now time to pull up.

Pull in.

Pile it up.

To gather gumption into herself.

These days, Martha often received hourly visits from her mother, some more gentle than others, that guided and propelled her to take steps of precious activity without falling into that lonely void where she had been sitting silent far too long.

The lonely days were over now.

It was time to fight once again.

Cypress beckoned Martha back into those moments, a current of memories that would carry her into the sphere of now.

The present.

No more living in the past but bringing the past to meet its gift of the present.

A gift of knowledge more valuable than the wealth of all kingdoms built by men.

A gift of lessons learned in time—a space that existed only for those who were living. Because the dead knew that time was as much a false notion as the credit garnered by years of toil on the backs of some for the profit of others.

But now, time was placed on her side.

Nothing had been lost.

Only gained.

As long as Cypress remained there by her side, Martha vowed she would not fail. She would succeed. And of that, she felt certain. If not for herself or her brothers, she would do so for Cypress and Jinn and Salome, and all who had come before them.

Martha at last burgeoned a will to fight, and she did so with a determination not unlike the strength she knew from her mother's spirit. She would give her all.

Let it loose!

Negro Law of South Carolina
Slaves, Their Civil Rights, Liabilities, and Disabilities

DeBow's Commercial Review

SEC. 20. The Acts of 1821 and 1841, are eminently wise, just, and humane. They protect slaves, who dare not raise their own hands in defense, against brutal violence. They teach men, who are wholly irresponsible in property, to keep their hands off the property of other people. They have wiped away a shameful reproach upon us, that we were indifferent to the lives or persons of our slaves. They have had too, a most happy effect on slaves themselves. They know *now,* that the shield of the law is over them; and thus protected, they yield a more hearty obedience and effective service to their masters.

Two things were left behind the day of the Blue invasion.

Cypress.

Cotton.

They would always be more connected and so much more valuable than anyone knew back then.

It was only much later that the assessment of such luck would come to light. Whether the windfall was for Cypress and the other human property abandoned that day—the day the Blues came and the planters fled with their families—or just all about the Northern coffers, only time would tell.

Salome's baby, Cypress, was born free on a blue day, and she did not believe at first the Blue soldier who told her so. In any event, Salome's legacy was Cypress and cotton. It was only later the land was thrown in.

Somehow Salome knew then, with her head swirled around the baby and the replacement of a plantation master by a Quartermaster, that some things never change, while others sneak up and push you over. Push you over in surprise as your world somehow upends.

Only much, much later would it be understood that the real fight her heirs would undertake would be not for the acres but for the water.

Ol Conjur had said this, but he had been laughed at and poohed by ol Granny and others.

Water only good for bringing more of us and bales to them, ol Granny had said.

Perhaps the cotton had been as impermanent as the feeling Salome had when she peered down at her bundle of autonomy.

Cypress had scared her so in the first years.

For all her cracked and broken ways, Salome knew Cypress would be one whole thing that was good and veracious and free. She would see to that. It was her duty, and no Missus or ol Granny had to tell her such.

She just knew it was so by looking at her.

∅

The Attorney was a she. The Attorney was a white woman.

Blonde, brassy, and brusque.

Yet somehow, Martha began to accept her. Took her in without resistance, in time.

Long over her initial shock from their first meeting, Martha settled slowly into a colonial captain's chair, and the Attorney reached to assist her before returning behind a monstrous oak desk.

At the left were framed photographs that covered almost the entire east wall, and as Martha studied them all, she grew more certain of the meeting and the possibility of trust in this white lady.

While their interaction seemed out of place here, the photo collage told her otherwise.

There the Attorney stood next Dr. King himself in front of what Martha recognized as the Penn Center, white shirtsleeves rolled up on his dark arms next to hers, as stark white as today.

Other faces in the photo were familiar to her somehow, but she could not place them. The Attorney was one of only two whites in the photograph, and it was a much younger version of her waving, smiling, boarding a bus.

And then there she was again with a group of women Martha's age or older. *Sea Island First Baptist Church, 1968*, it said on the inscription below it.

Voter registration, the placard read.

She seen some things, Martha now had no doubt.

"Hello, Mrs. Planter, how wonderful to see you again," the Attorney started in.

"Called my brother in Chicago to make better sense of what you have told me," Martha said, buoyed by their mutual strokes.

Double-blessed.

The Attorney was relieved by not having to begin again. To start over with explanations she gave daily to those who likely understood but filtered her words through habitual distrust of her race. A distrust deep as skin and vernacular and so great that most never got past it.

But Martha had been different. The Attorney had first met her at the prayer meeting with Reverend Saul, who had introduced them.

Martha had been so timid and meek, the Attorney had dialed down her usual aggression and taken greater care with her words when speaking to this woman, who was clearly stronger than she first appeared. She would soon win her over.

The Attorney had not seen Martha since that first time she had stumbled into her office, waving the document, wailing like a mother mourning a child graveside, falling into a chair in the waiting area, not sure who would show up to save her.

Happened again.
Coming for us again.
Help us.

CYPRESS

By the time the first school had opened for the newly-freed island souls, Cypress was almost walking but too young to learn to read, and Salome thought she herself was too late, too old. But age mattered little when the Blue General ensured her that she had received a plot of land, same as the other freedmen.

A plot of Tabby Place no less.

Men never had enough, Salome had known well before she was hauled up in a burlap bag every time she had resisted Master Planter, just like the day he had picked her.

Her childlike parts were on display for all to see.

"Clean her up and put her with the other pretty one. They will appraise better together," were the only words she could recall from the shapeless gruff voices that had turned her this way and that.

Prepared her for viewing.

∅

Master Planter's high-octave tone was gone, but at first, the similar gravel in the General's pitchy voice had almost comforted her. He had let Salome continue to reside in a room off the kitchen house while he and his regiment moved into the rest after Salome birthed Cypress.

Like the tabby cat that owned the kitchen house, Salome was not about to give her baby up, and she would scratch out the eyes of anyone who tried to take her.

Soldier, no soldier.

Gun, no gun. No matter.

Ol Granny stayed put to guard Salome as she instructed the General. Both were needed.

They would see.

Best butter biscuits ever, she bartered.

They were not leaving home.

Even if viewed as level with the dirt where Tabby Place existed. Master Planter had thought Sea Island dirt was worth much more.

And for some unearthly reason, the grayed man in the tattered blue coat seemed to be listening to ol Granny.

Even saw her. Tapped her as if in comfort.

Now, now, he had said softly.

No one's leaving here now.

Ø

Of course, by 1899 there were no more 160-pound yields to be had, and 40-times-18 cents did not require numeracy beyond basic arithmetic to understand that there was no longer a living to be scraped from the cotton plant.

By then, Cypress had garnered the purse strings and learned all the lessons she needed to know—at least those to be had from Jinn's handling of dollars and coins for the basics—long before the babies came.

No more.

From then on, she would rule her house with an ironed-out grip on their necks and instill what she had learned in them; she would teach them the strength of life near death, lest they needed it to save their own sometime.

It was never any easier.

Only different.

She would find their way.

Too late to give up on this land.

∅

The school teacher said it so softly that Salome did not understand for sure and was too afraid to speak up and ask what it was that they had for Cypress.

The Blues had been followed by more.

Teachers. Missionaries. Nurses. Abolitionists. Schools and churches were built.

Your daughter will learn to read as you have, the teacher repeated. *She will learn to write. Will be easier for her as a child,* the teacher explained.

Kind she was, so patient for a white woman.

Easier for her; she has always been free, Salome corrected.

Cypress born free. She would not let them forget.

Ancient Shell Rings

Thomas Glutton, *South Carolina Historical Society*

On Sea Island, there lie ancient shell rings some have considered to be at least 3,000 years old. Members of the early Woodland nation, whose partial sustenance was the rich shellfish of the island, may have lived within the circular pattern and discarded their refuse around the ring circumference of several hundred feet, as pottery, charcoal, and other artifacts have been found to be crushed within the shell structure. Other interpretations have considered the shell rings, which rose to as high as 10 feet in places, to be ancient ceremonial or worship enclaves. In either event, antebellum plantation owners quarried the site to create tabby for building purposes, leaving the sites poorly excavated, incomplete, and sadly unprotected until now.

They knew it was wrong.

They were sensitive to the sacred circles, but choice was not a part of action back then. Having a choice meant you had a will and a purpose and actions driven beyond another. When choice is not a consideration, action is taken without thought and likely with mandate that holds behind it all the consequences you know you do not want to ever see.

Choice would only come much, much later; it was never seen in the days of those who had come first and poured the tabby mansion for the Captain.

It had been a task for the strong backs who had arrived first and learned quickly to save those backs through silence and action. That was the way of those early survivors, ol Granny had explained, as she had watched them through the port window where, too often now, Salome saw the rocking waves of an ocean rather than moss-hung trees.

By the time Salome came, the tabby had long been poured solid as the walls of the island house that confined her to strokes on the fine dishes that defined her role once she came out from behind skirts and wore her own beauty like the guile of her namesake.

The mistaken one who had powers to protect her own. Only later would she have choice and take action that unfolded like the hurricane that came much, much later, when they were all working the land as it were their own. Given to them in the Blue invasion, then taken back. Choice was all she wished for the little one, and decisions like this shifted with each hour that it grew inside her.

The outbuildings were the last to be constructed and, by happenstance, came to be the last to hold when the Blues came. But that was to be much later, and this was still the old time when cotton could not stop the bleeding and rice paddies were where the fungus and snakes that left ricers hobbled and the pickers bleeding out grew. The horrors she encountered in the house were just different and could not be compared to the wounds of the others.

Salome gave her head a quick shake and lost those thoughts and whispers that only brought kicks and slaps before she knew it. Missus Planter had a quick temper and an even quicker slap when it came to Salome. She knew of her husband's affection for the female and it had never bothered her with the others, but for some reason this one had gotten under her skin, and even she was ashamed of her unevenness when it came to abusing these women who were hers to care for her and her home. Why she felt this way, she never understood, except that perhaps there was a beauty in what she usually saw as dirty and indecent, and hidden underneath it all, when no one was watching, even she could acknowledge the attraction to her house girl that she did not understand.

By the time Salome carried Cypress, the protective feeling conflicted with Missus Planter's usual attitude toward those who served her, and this made her somehow want to beat Salome all the more. And if she admitted it further, she wanted to tear at her skin and her belly and carve out this thing that did not belong to Salome but to her. It was hers too, whatever this infant might be, boy or girl; it would belong to her and would serve her, and she detested the curved, shielding hand that Salome held over her belly.

"You just wait and see when that baby is snatched from you and raised to be his house child," she would whisper to Salome.

"Don't you tilt that head to him," she said as she tooled her words into the finest point possible to stab into Salome's ear.

When Salome let her hovering hand touch the convection of her belly even slightly, it was too much for Missus Planter to see, and she reacted more than she wanted to, but it was almost as if she could not stop herself. She had to punish Salome for her connection with this child she carried.

An infant always followed the womb, and therefore, whether boy or girl, this baby would be born a slave, documented as chattel of the Planters, and would be their own. How dare Salome touch her belly as if somehow, she would own this child when the fact was the Planters might sell it as soon as it was weaned from her. Prize or no prize, lust or no lust, it would be Missus Planter who would make this decision and not her husband. She governed the house females, and she would decide their fate. This she reminded Salome as often as she could and whenever she saw the touch grow in this selfishness.

"Not now, Salome."

Her words would whack harder than the backhandedness with which she inflicted both.

The day of the Blue invasion, Salome did not bow her head when she saw Missus Planter's hand coming at her but turned her face full square and risked a look directly into the Missus' eyes. A full-on gaze knocked her back with a quick gasp, and Missus Planter pulled both hands to her chest as if to protect her heart from whatever contempt this defiance delivered. As the sun reached its golden half circle on the beach horizon that evening, Salome had changed. She was committed to it and would never again let anyone knock her down.

∅

It was the next day that the Blues came with their ships and guns and knives. Salome had never seen terror in Master Planter's eyes like that blue morning. Oh, there were days when the cotton looked scully or the rice molded, and he had an anger traced with worry, yes, but it was never this sort of horror. His wide eyes almost matched ol Granny's when she got slapped by Missus Planter for simply acting old when of course it was no act at all if a slap could keep it at bay.

Missus Planter always slapped because she could, and ol Granny always pretended as though it had not touched her. Ol Granny was the first to smile; she had never seen them pack and run so fast all by themselves.

No help was asked for, but the yelling made up for that. This was no seasonal escape to the inland summer home. This was life or death, and flight was the only path open to life.

Salome smiled to herself that there was none of that haughty secessionist talk today. Where was the arrogant flip and slap across her thigh now? Swept away with Missus Planter in her careless packing.

All gone at the sight of blue.

At the fright of blue.

The bluest Blue ol Granny had ever seen.

It was a terrifying Blue that brought Missus Planter to her knees in loud prayer, as if she deserved to be lifted up now and cared for like a precious babe. A babbling babe, that was what she became, and it made Salome hang on even tighter to the newborn bundle Cypress was then. She was a wriggler, as though she wanted to see everything that was happening, all that she had brought with her.

Then, like the flash of the overseer's whip on a beaten man's haughty soul: gone.

Even Salome came out of her after-birth stupor to peer out at all the terrified faces and lay her head back in awe.

She brought it.

She did.

Ol Granny whispered to Salome and to anyone in the house within earshot of her musty, guttural lisp. That whisper propped them up for the change, and they were relieved when they heard it—and less guilty for ignoring the bobbing of a silver chicken, left headless and writhing on the chop block.

She brought it.

It's done.

The Planter family never returned to the island after the day the Blues arrived, but they were not the last to find or to own it. Salome assumed charge of the land that had once ruled her, and so long as she handled its reins and kept a keen eye fixed on the horizon, nothing would pitch her footing from those fields.

No one would get in or out.

So much so that it would be years before Salome ever believed she was free to leave the island, and then, of course, it would only be because of Cypress.

MARTHA

Martha was not a woman of regret in any traditional sense. Oh yes, she pined for lost love, a sister who never was, the lost children of her siblings, her own children who were never to be.

Normal regrets hardly worth the notice when there was so much to do.

And silent regrets that came as pastoral connections to tourists and beachers who arrived in droves.

It was the latter silent regrets that plagued her more. Sunset destroyers that sought her out in weakness. Especially in those rare times when she dropped her guard. Especially in her garden, among the well-cultivated kale and vinca.

It was in the few moments before sleep, when she thought rest would never come and she tried to let down her mind's armor in the dark, that those thoughts would spear her with their spikes and shards, which she had been able to fight off in the daylight.

Cut her up alive in her just-before-sleep drifting as if they were there with her right then.

Sleep was her only escape, and she would do anything to reach it.

Martha and Kenneth never married officially, but she used his family name—Bailey—to hide Planter, and they had no children of their own. They raised her cousin's child for a time, and while Kenneth's father told them there was no shame in that, they had done it solely because the child's mother worked.

Work was a great redeemer even then.

Yet as time went on, the child's mother began frequenting the creekside juke joint, and that brought shame on Martha and the child. So much so that the child's mother was banished from Freetown, and the last anyone heard, she had made her way South to Florida.

Good riddance, they all said.

Martha understood her parcel. She read its legal description again and again until the pages outlining her dirt were worn from her thumb pads gripping hard next to the paragraph.

At nine years old, her brother Simon had trained under the old carpenter, Hemmy, who had taught him the sheathing and plugging way to build things. It took more time, but time had no value back then. Only problem was, Simon was impatient and enamored with time's interruptions. He never could claim himself an artisan because he had no patience for the time needed to make something lasting.

He cut corners.

He burned through projects that required a light, patient touch. But the burn in his soul would not allow it—he could not lose himself within it—and a craftsman he would never be.

They all should have seen this early on but didn't.

Not even Cypress.

When a seed was planted and took root, a life force returned to earth with all of the glory and promise of a new day. This was the story that Jinn had told them as babies, and now they lived it.

Maybe not in his way but in a new way. It was the new day that Martha lived for in her dreams, where she imagined this was what Cypress had wanted for them.

For all of them.

To continue on.

Hold on.

Cotton gave them all the backbreaking work they needed. But then weevils came and ran off all the planters who thought they could emulate the old times and see cotton pave the way for the land's future generations in white hues, wide and low and enduring.

The sun would set, supper would be eaten, and at last Martha would lie down, close her eyes, and find that escape. A new day found her now that she was no longer alone.

Useless though she was, she was all there was now.

You can't understand where you're headed if you don't know where you came from, Martha decided, and she would be the one to tell all of them so.

Hers was the future, and she would see to it that she propelled it forward.

All of it.

She was the only chance she had now for Cypress to subsist, so she would have to do.

Like it or not, she had been dealt.

They had left her on her own with her visions and aspirations, as if they felt no connection to what had been before.

She knew this was not actually true, but it sure appeared so.

They had simply given up.

More simply, they'd had nowhere else to go but north.

Yet Martha was no quitter.

She had a job to do here.

It was here that she belonged.

Here she would stay.

And no county official was going to tell her she did not belong here.

She would rouse that angry spark in this whitewashed urban façade and see it ignite. She had seen it unsettled there under her elder brother's buttoned-up attire.

Martha usually judged a person by their shoes. It was the shoes that gave clues as to the soul that resided underneath. Truman wore those smooth, black two-inch heels, the ones of a street vendor or saxophonist, that collided with the rest of the tight, urban plaid. Those heels did not belong on an unadventurous spirit, she decided immediately the day she met the Attorney, and those shoes gave Martha a glimpse into the red-hot soul underneath all her reasonable show. She would show her brothers. If they would not come back, she would win this on her own.

The Attorney did not know it yet, but she too would come to hear the wail Cypress had left here, where her spirit had walked and left a trail for the land's successors.

Martha knew no one could squelch the flame of Cypress's wail once it had sparked an uprising. It burned through, illuminating the land and giving its inhabitants something—anything—to hang on to.

The first time Martha heard Cypress after her body gave up, she heard a yowl that she would never forget.

Beyond breathing.

Beyond seething.

It was a force that ran up the trees and down the shoreline and surrounded the island with an energy so palpable it gave off warmth.

Heat, really.

Yes, it was like a sun in some ways, and yet there it was, situated in that too-big old white moon that hovered over the black waves, telling them something.

A message.

Meaning. Memory.

It sent words like lightning bolts up Martha's spine, splitting her head wide open with recognition when the time came to grasp that inner strength for herself.

Hold on.

Eyes wide open.

Sit up straight.

Proud.

It certainly lit up Martha on those dark, dank nights when she raged out into the inky marsh at her brothers: those quitters. Who had given in, given up, run up, and settled for some row house in Charleston or Chicago.

All the same, North or South.

Scrunched together like sturgeon packed in a too-tight smoker.

It was not so much this parcel, with its ground and garden for leisure and its single section of the Tabby Place field for planting, as it was their unscrupulous nature. They had simply left it for what they thought was better.

Better days.

Better life.

Maybe they had never heard the lesson quite as clear as she had as a small child, back when Cypress had still been with them and cradled Martha in the same chair as Salome had done for her. Martha heard it now as clear as then. It softened her when she got too rough. It made her more rugged when she turned dull, bolstered her when she fell into the bleakness surrounding her and present in the puddles of neighbors, so easy to step into rather than across whenever she became careless.

Yes, Martha had learned to use what Cypress left.

What she had left within her.

When it came down to it, she blamed Simon less, really, because she had expected more of Truman. They all had. He'd had all of the same lessons from Cypress, but he had squandered his energy on something less. Once their last cotton crop had been lost, he'd followed his lust to the Lowcountry. He'd begun to read those awful rags from the North, and Martha had watched his passion dissipate right out the top of his head, and the vigor with which he once had held so tightly alongside her began to fade.

Jobs, he'd said over and over.
Paid job.

His departure would not be any different from so many of the others, Truman told himself, letting that engine drive him north to escape suffocation. By a suffering that could not be erased by oyster netting or a shrimp trawler. Unlike for Simon, the drink had not worked for Truman when he was younger, so it was not going to help his escape now.

He went North to determine his own course. At least that showed he still had some of the old gumption Cypress had seen in him.

By then, he had shut his eyes and ears to anything intangible and decided it was the hard, cold steel of the North that he could latch onto.

Hard. Cold. Real.

That was where he would know what to do.

One day, Truman simply stopped speaking of dirt, fertilizer, and cultivation of seed as life. No more of Cypress's words came from his lips. Instead his mind locked in on payments and prices. And once a man had done that, there was no going back to the germinations of dreams or soul-bound notions.

Dollar had taken hold of him, and he was going to seek it. He was committed to finding that 'somewhere else' that could only be found after his abandonment of the island that had shown him only adversity: widespread pain, too few cents, the torment he could no longer stomach.

Simon was already gone by then anyway, Truman would remind Martha later at graveside, when he'd had to say goodbye to Cypress that last time. He could not have left without offering his final respects, his parting gesture providing one more dose of encouragement for Martha. Least he had that.

"So what's the use?" he'd said, brushing Martha's appeals aside, packing as furiously as if he was being chased out.

"It's yours too." She had stoked and goaded his new desire.

In this together.

She would gnash desperate words.

Hang on to the dirt.

It was all of their dirt.

She had harped on too furiously, spilling her bidding words over and over and over into the closed, deafened ears of Cypress's oldest son, the firstborn who wanted no more of this life.

This place. This land.

Door closed.

Yet here it was, open again, bringing with it a fresh calling for Martha.

An offering of sorts.

One more chance to hold on.

One more chance to not do this alone.

A chance to hold, again.

An heir.

That meant something.

Really, it meant everything.

∅

Martha told Truman the Attorney had said the property title was *foggy*.

No, maybe she had said *cloudy*.

She shook her head fiercely, angry at her own hazy memory. The legal terms confused her, although she knew inherently what it all meant.

When they had first shown her the title in Salome's singular name, it was impossible for Martha to explain, drowning in the voices of Salome through Cypress now solely hers.

Salome Planter was scrawled in a beautiful, illegible line that drew the matrilineal path of images dancing among her now: Jinn and Blues and water and hovering spirits and ships and parallel shacks with twice-sized, neatly-hoed rows, white hoods, government checks, and weevil-shredded cotton that had tattered so many pockets and purses and souls.

Stories she had heard from her mother over a lifetime. For it was a pedigree that would be even more sordid if she did not protect it. Rein it back in.

Cypress had told her this day would come.

Her turn now.

∅

'Leave and never set foot' was what Simon had shouted when Martha lost herself fireside many a night.

Never set foot!

Later, the quiet time was disrupted by the North once again, when some guilty descendent of a rice planter decided to put broke islanders to work on a causeway built entirely by manual labor.

When the Developer had shown up at the church information meeting four years later, the laborers had turned around with elbow nudges and confirmed old suspicions.

Opportunist Bridge, they had called it back then.

"For all of us," the Developer had said, spreading his hands out in a beautiful fan, palms upraised to the heaven like John the Baptist up to his knees in the river.

The ricer's great-grandson had stood next to him, nodding, palm over hand, crossed and respectful like a stoic Sunday usher.

For all of us.

'Never leave us be' was muttered, but paid work was paid work.

∅

The linkages within the family were burning her like an overseer's tight cuff, marking her, forcing her to spill it out into the present light of day simply for the relief that came from such release. Martha felt this for sure even though she had never been cuffed but instead had felt the chafe of Salome's wrists upon her own.

Chained up. Chained down.

Chained arm-in-arm but with an unexpected collective force that could not be contained any longer.

Cypress had been freed, and it had been released because of that.

Jinn's stories swirled around her head, and she saw it all as it had been then.

A glimpse. A chance.

A moment to believe that the broken chains would remain as such.

It was a story that had smoldered long enough within her.

It might take the rest of her lifetime to tell it right.

Set it right.

Martha was unsure just exactly how long that meant. Or more accurately, how long she had left to accomplish the duty that had been left to her.

All she knew for sure was that when it began to emerge from her, she might be set ablaze.

Spontaneous combustion.

It was that red and hot and fiery, and it would consume her eventually, that much she was sure of, but first she had to get it out of herself and share it with this Attorney she hardly knew before her time ran out.

All her desperate and pleading letters to Truman that she'd thought had gone unread.

Perhaps it would always matter when it came to land ownership in this Lowcountry that had pushed away all its sons along with her two brothers who had run North, buoyed by the resistance they felt, to make something of what had never been theirs by name. It had certainly been paid for by a bloodline they would soon forget in a northern net of safety.

A new start for each, but only one had lasted.

The other brother was lost somewhere, running from the past, running toward no future. Blinded by a pain of indeterminate origin.

A boy once, a boy still.

Martha felt Simon sometimes, wounded and howling somewhere. She would give anything to find him now, to console her lost brother who was not to blame but had been the start of war.

She had known for some time that neither brother, broken and patched up in their own ways, would ever come back, but she had no idea that the elder would send her the gift of his son in his stead.

Blessed was all she could think at the time.

Blessed.

Martha remembered those speckled cheeks and deep-set eyes of Jinn's—the wisest old man she had ever known.

Land is freedom, Cypress had once told her.

Martha tried starting again with a line she had heard so often from Cypress that she felt it run up and down her arms with the tingling responsibility Cypress had passed on to her care. She was afraid the words would not come and that she would never have the fire to convey them as her mother had.

It was too much. Simply too much to tell all at once.

So she would parse it out carefully for this wise-eyed Attorney. It was now her duty to see to it that she fueled it in order to break wide the line drawn across an ocean to an island to her heart and to all of the ghosts that surrounded them now.

Pleading. Pleading through her now.

She was a lonely old witless woman that Cypress had somehow left with this burden, and her brothers had run off and left only her. She had been left to carry on.

Yet here she was now. A miracle.

∅

The Developer's people had found a naïve prospect in Jolene.

She had already tired of turning spirals in a hair salon off Troy in Weeksville since completing her cosmetic certificate a few months earlier, before anyone cared whether Weeksville had history. She was scared into half-wits when two suited-up white men entered the shop.

The shop owner said, "What you want?" but they ignored her and knew Jolene in her funked-out dress on sight.

Took her right then to the corner diner and laid out the plan in simple dollars and cents; anyone could have understood.

She thought she had won a street-craps wager and bragged up and down till word got back to Simon's old Harlem street pals, now wiser in business themselves, and they sent news on back home to the island.

Martha was warned well ahead that something bad was coming, long before she'd telephoned Truman, but they'd left out the fact that Simon had fathered her a niece and kept such secrets up north where they belonged.

Had not even shared that Simon was long dead, buried by the county in some pauper's grave nowhere known nor seen.

That's how it was in those days when one lost touch. They all had their reasons.

Keep it quiet. Keep it north.

No one was happier than Jolene, except her mother, of course. Helena, who still had lines to her people down South now that she had changed, dropped her junk and praised the Lord. *Forgiven her old ways but not forgotten what was rotten*, as they said back home.

Islanders knew Helena would drop anything for a whiff of dolla' and all that it brought to her mind's eye.

She packed up Jolene, left her longshore rat behind, and headed back south quick as could be, bunking in with cousin Nama and the kids. Old man had since left her anyhow, so she had the room.

The Developer's people prepared Jolene well for what was at stake, feeding her and her mother, even sending fruit baskets to Nama and the kids, a pittance for now with the big payday to come.

Wait. Patience.

Dressed her up for the part.

Decided in court soon. Very soon.
All well worth the wait.

∅

Back then, after cotton was over, there were those that headed north, and upon seeing their old workmates along the main roads and back-roads, forgot where they were headed, so they turned 'round to come back to what they knew.

Those that kept going were another sort, who somehow saw money to be made elsewhere, and if they did go back, their pockets were full.

By Cypress's funeral, Martha knew Truman had made out okay, but Simon had never had much luck, and later she lost his trail.

SALOME

The females in the kitchen quarters were forced to be sisters of a sort.

Not kin.

No blood tied them.

Yet decidedly sisters.

Bound together out of domesticity and tied up with the faux privilege that was enclosed within the house's walls. A fortunate few who had seen the others banished, sent off to the gruels, which they knew none could endure.

Beyond survival, really.

Had these women not had each other, they would not have existed beyond the machinations of their arms and legs and sometimes their innards, constrained to doing work unfit for the slender fingers and soft palms it would render lined and scaled. Sucked dry of oils and vested in a drought that could not be watered.

Memories blotted out under a sunrise and sunset that still reminded them of the far-off place from which they had first drifted. Glimpses in the mind's eye, then merely afforded luxuries, were paid for with a rap to the shoulder or hand, or worse, as Salome had paid.

Sisters in a sense besting any bloodline, Salome thought as she looked over at the woman she had come to think of as her mother during her time there. Their real mothers and sisters were long gone on a ship packed tight like a sardine liner basking in oils but with nowhere near as much room. Sisters in a sense that made no sense except to help them carry on their work chin down. They were bound as if by blood, since choice was not a consideration for any of them.

It was what it was back then.

Ol Granny touched Salome's belly ever so lightly, as if offering a silent blessing while they worked over biscuits and greens, and quietly said it.

Cypress.

The baby had already been named the night before in the old way by ol Conjur, and all the next day, Salome held tightly to her baby's

tradition-christened name. She could not tell if it was ol Conjur's long-
ing or an actual incantation that had slipped out uncontrolled from his
old, pursed lips, but she knew she must accept such a gift. It was the
old way, and it did not always come so easily anymore.

When the music comes, you simply accept it.
Own it.
Possess it, or it will possess you.

Salome had taken this phrase for keeps back then, an old thought
that was long ago walled up with many others, harbored away from
the daylight of her mind, as she no longer dared to listen to them.
Kept locked up even when it was merely comfort she sought. But this
thought carried the stronger voice of the dead, sounded just like the
closed, tight voice back on the ship that whispered all the lessons she
had clung to when she'd first crossed and would clutch even more firmly if ever she could make them out.

But she no longer dreamed this dream.

Salome, listen.
I tell you these things to carry.
You are a carrier.
You will carry them for all of us.

Salome touched her belly ever so lightly, the slight gesture willed by
the remembered thoughts, and quickly realized her error the moment
she felt the hand whack against the back of her head.

Loaded again, you old cow!
Leave your belly be!

She bent her head back over the russets and shook it back and
forth, back and forth, to say silently that she would never again be
tender to herself in that way.

Such a narrow world she inhabited.

Perhaps it was because her mother had kept her world so small, had
kept it secure and manageable.

Manageable solely within bounds that one could see.

Could feel.

Predict.

For, if it were up to her to escape it, she would surely lose control. She had only lost control once before, and she'd assured herself that it would never happen again.

She would teach her daughter how to keep the boundaries always within sight. Use the gift like her mother, the all-knowing world that could be seen, touched, and felt.

Tight.

Within reach.

It was better this way.

The cool Lowcountry breeze came in April, toting the promise of warm on the way and sweltering after that.

And Salome lifted her head, something rarely done.

She lost herself, immersed in the full gale against her hairline, and turned to let it reach her neck, brush over the nape that never cooled, graze the underside of the upturned chin that never trembled.

Then she bent.

Head down again.

Not daring to believe the false encouragement of the April coolness, for she knew she would only be disappointed come June, when the hot, dense air would strangle her and the work would not allow her to lift her head again.

Master Planter always grunted when he was done.

Bent down.

Held down.

It was better this way. It was the strength of her mind that never departed her, that never betrayed her sight. She kept it to herself during her work, and after, when she washed away the duty of her privilege and Missus Planter forcefully splatted her face, she was only knocked down the first time.

And then, as she pressed on, she accepted rebuke, strong and as she should, letting it burn her innards and scald her lining and allowing absolutely no one to see that she was moved.

It was the first time that she always would remember. When she had felt the force of life rise within her, had forced herself to shelve it alongside the jars that lined the cookhouse walls.

She'd looked at it above her. Within reach.

Separate. Removed.

And even if it was for just a moment, the cookhouse's hot and pungent congestion had seemed to subside.

One day, Salome knew she would reach for that force.

Bring her will back and secure it. Place it within her once more to carry her home.

But back then, it had been better that way.

∅

Martha began with her mother's words. "This land is our freedom."

She slow-paced the rest. "But don't think of it as our own. We are the caretakers and must protect it. There is no amount of money worth giving it up. We are the caretakers and must hang on."

The Attorney understood. Blood and time, licks of a near past she could never understand, the bounds of a waking life that never slept in this South.

Surely Cypress ran in her veins now—a rush Martha could feel.

Truman had been sleepwalking too, till now.

"Wake up!" she willed her brother in her mind.

Then, like the jolt of a forgotten task remembered, Martha felt a new confidence fill her, and she knew she was no longer alone.

Ours.

"We will do this together," she declared aloud, and the Attorney nodded.

"Together," the Attorney concurred.

We will do this together.

∅

The Captain was a wayward sailor turned trader of the best sort.

He knew his cargo would ultimately save an island that would otherwise be uninhabitable. Like his father before him, a war hero of the utmost character and integrity, it was this high regard of self that would serve him best.

His daddy had seen to that.

Beat him down.

Built him up.

That had been the motto used to turn the lazy, moody son into a leader of men. If only the Captain had turned away from the card table in his younger years, perhaps a fortune could have been amassed, but he had no willpower when it came to wagers.

Yet the Captain also knew these waterways like the back of his roughhewn hand. He had no need for Charleston middlemen who bit off profit for simple willingness to do the in-between dirty work.

No, the Captain would do his trading directly with planters. It was better this way and most certainly more rewarding.

He had found a need, and he would fill it.

Simple economics.

The Captain had bought ol Conjur from a neighbor when the soothsayer had still been a young man and a bit more unwieldy with his gift.

That was long before Master Planter had assumed him, with the certificate for all of the property, when he had won Tabby Place off the Captain in that legendary poker hand.

The loss still bit into him at times, but a seaman had no use for dirt anyhow.

Ol Conjur had always wished to remain with the Captain, since he knew, better than most, what lay ahead with Master Planter.

Slap. Slap, slap.

Shake. Shake, shake, and done.

The Captain had shared secrets, sought the guidance that ol Conjur was known to provide, and he'd wished Master Planter well with his winnings once he'd sobered up and decided he was more fit for the sea than the failed indigo he' ultimately had to relinquish.

The Captain was no farmer.

So foolish of him to think he could master the land when his soul was honed, refined, and called daily by water. Movement was in his blood, and he would not own land if he had no station in it.

Good riddance!

The land, though a sea island, was not for him. And back on a boat, he sailed where he could battle what he knew best; this helped him to leave the island. All would be well once the bank released his debt and cleared the deed transfer to Master Planter, who simply added it to his collection of inherited acres, never thinking twice about moving his family to this desolate wintering place.

That was as of the day of settling, anyway, and even ol Conjur could not have predicted that far into the future.

Some things are best left behind the veil, but when a man is young, he does not see that restraint is not always for the weakest.

The Captain had never listened back then anyway. He'd heard the bits and snips he wanted and left the rest to the future to unfold on its own.

This time, ol Conjur stood his full height, making the sign of the cross with both hands—the Captain always mistook this for a full conversion from the hoodoo—and peering through it as he viewed the Captain's east-parting ship.

You will fail.

Believe it.

Ol Conjur jumped back then so as to avoid any wide whacks from the Captain; he knew what would come in the onslaught of any cold, hard, coarse words he could use to reject a negative forecast, especially this one. The one he had been running from for years on end.

He was tired, and perhaps it had finally caught him, but still he could not let on that he believed such a truth.

The whack was as weak as his old sea legs, and the Captain's words had lost their bite, turned almost to a plea as he wiped ol Conjur's face with them, knowing full well they did not grab hold of any part of the now-decrepit old seer.

Ol Conjur knew better than to smirk in front of this broken man, even though he saw that he could have gotten away with it this time. Instead, pity crept in and bubbled up his windpipe like the dearth from the old place, a sad, wailing song of hunger and loss used to revive the spirit of fortune.

It was a mourning strain no one here would even hum anymore, as fortune had remained across the water. And it had not come looking for them when they left the home water and the lost-east shore became a speck in the mind's eye as they avoided the gritty eyes of captors with their blunts.

But fail he did.

The Captain, who could never refuse the sight of a card table when he was on dry ground, would never profit from the most lucrative crop the South had ever seen, for his failure preceded the land's success.

He had lost the fields and his partners.

Dead before the first bales of cotton even left Savannah to become the Queen's most luxurious bedsheets

And still more.

All that anyone ever wanted was more of the luxuriance that came from hands they never had to look at, hands encumbered with sleeplessness and toil to provide their benefactors with an antidote to the insomnia their restless hands could not escape.

Sea Island Cotton was to come as a boon never before seen—before Cypress, that was—and only the most cynical would ever propose that it had carried with it the island's fatidic spell. And as for the rest, it was mostly happenstance, even though luck back then was for more than just the fortunate. It was a reminder that misfortune could become an embattled soul but could not wrestle away the small bit of fight from that soul or the wisp of hope that someone would see.

Grab on.

The unrest and its subsequent release began to rule the island. And no logical man could ever blame Cypress for bringing all that.

Yet when she did come, her arrival disrupted what some believed would go on forever.

And disruption, of course, can be good, bad, or a mix of both, depending upon who's looking.

∅

Even ol Granny steered clear of her till she gave birth, when Cypress appeared and changed it all forever.

Cypress came with a howl that cut clean through the pre-dawn and woke the sun. Such a glorious shriek reached all the way down to the souls still filtering at the water's edge in the places and spaces close enough to the bay that they could hear it.

Probably even made those moving beyond stay in close just a bit longer.

Never mind that she was half Planter.

Actually, no one really cared about that, as it was a glorious day, and, after all, she was a special child. That much was clear. An answer.

Cypress just didn't know it yet, as her baby soul had not yet caught sense.

"Oh, look away," they all said once she caught it. Cypress could bring the ocean right to the shore like no moon's tide ever had once she owned it.

Just wait.

Hope was not much of a commodity back then. No one then had the ability to see beyond what they could taste, touch, see, smell, or hear. No need to rile things up.

Only then came Cypress, and she was a bundle of hope from the get-go. And somehow, everyone knew it. It was to be her time, and something was about to change. How they ever managed to believe it after all that had happened since the old time, no one could say. But there she was, dropped in their midst with a racket as though carted in by some sort of divine right.

Forecast and right.

Resurrection fern
Polypodium polypodioides

Botany of the Low Country, E.M. Hicks, 1879

This non-native perennial is an air plant that attaches itself to other plants and gets its nutrients from the air and from water and nutrients that collect on the outer surface of bark. Resurrection fern lives on the branches of large trees such as cypresses and live oaks and is often the neighbor of Spanish moss and wild pine but has been known to inhabit up to eight or 10 species.

The fern is named so because it can survive long periods of drought by curling up and appearing dead. However, when water is present, the fern will uncurl and reopen as if resurrected. Certain royal botanists noted that the fern may have been used to heal boils and sores by the Lumbee natives.

It was to be a great social test, this port experiment. A first test of freedom.

By spring, Salome was glad she had actually stuck around because who knew where she might have landed, or her child for that matter. Perhaps both dead.

Instead, they now lived together, mama and baby. And the Blues had even let them remain in the cabin Master Planter had built for her near what was now Jinn's seed barn.

Two side-by-side secrets at the back of the big house.

Cypress no secret now. Jinn laughed as he snuck over whenever he could to see the beauty shining from her radiant face.

Ol Granny had named her for the tree and predicted three children for her based on the three-finger count of the tree's knees that poked through its marsh blanket. She had hid from Missus in the panic before the Blues reached the big house. Missus, who had given up in her search and taken kitchen Low instead.

Salome and ol Granny laughed over the cookery that must be nettling Missus in Beaufort and further unsettling Master Planter's chronic gastritis.

In the spring, the Quartermaster visited Salome again. bringing with him a young blond Blue with a great stride to walk off her plot.

Salome thought this new master wanted payment, so she shimmied him up and down with a smile, and he had none of it, which confused her altogether.

Actually shook his head.

Then she turned her smile on the blonde Blue, who blushed azalea-red and turned toward the Quartermaster seeking direction and safety.

Record the margins, the Quartermaster ordered.

Forty acres, give or take, were logged in the great land ledger in the parlor-turned-record room in the big house.

Salome Planter.

[Land owner.]

∅

Master Planter returned that second time and demanded his plantation acres, as most had been handed out to those who stayed, and then the causeway was built, and for the first time, there was more than ferry access to an inland they knew little of except to visit the courthouse, which typically occurred during an opportune life event or defeat.

Never really anything in between.

This single mother household was not incomplete, as some might say.

Cypress raised her children to live as they always had.

A simple shack that was expanded a few feet each direction with each child depending upon their month of birth.

North.

East.

West.

No South baby arrived for her.

There was to be no more South for the Planters.

Salome instructed her with the last name even when others were saying there was no need, but when the '70 census worker visited, she proudly declared it and told the worker there was no Mister Planter here.

She was head of household.

Like Salome, Cypress never left her brood till she could breathe no more. Martha could scarcely remember the solemn funeral parade from the church to the edge water that day.

Without Cypress, there was no reason for Kenneth to stick around for Martha. In his mind, anyway. *Better things to do than this lonely life*, he told Truman the last time they spoken.

Others said Kenneth headed to Georgia and found his way north up to Virginia, but all that was just runners' gossip. Still others blamed Martha.

Those women too proud, some said. *Menfolk just can't stick by that.*

TRUMAN

It was the humble-looking sign that had first embedded itself somewhere into his unconscious, sparking memories he'd had no idea even existed until he'd arrived at that very long week. Truman drove through a cluster of manufactured homes—mobile homes, they said up north—and saw the poorly-painted slab of pulpwood: *Freetown*.

This overdue family reunion was certainly not attended by choice. Truman was reluctant (or grateful) and had first sent a letter.

No. Better left to handle on her own.

Some reunions are just not meant to happen.

At that point, of course, he could not have known how the disquiet would overtake him year by year. Consume him. Almost devour him.

He'd considered the stories mere words, and no amount of the history Martha had encroached with could have changed the orderly days of his life back then.

Whatever the reason, though, Martha's recounts of his heritage had compelled Truman to return here.

It was the *future* that had mattered when he first went north. That had seen him through.

Work hard. Best one can be.

Made it our own way. Worked for it.

No chins on the hands. Chin up. Good and solid.

Feet on the ground.

You will see. You will see.

Now he was home, and all his stable and sturdy northern life seemed just ash.

Pure ash.

Never really solid at all.

When he first arrived, Martha's trailer had appeared an exoskeleton of sorts.

That was the only way Truman could describe the conglomeration it had become. He sucked a quick drag from a Camel stub for any possible relief he could gain from the smoke. He typically did not partake in cigarettes, and yet upon arriving here, he somehow could do not otherwise. The old neighbors all smoked, and Truman felt sort of awkward not doing so. He'd bought a pack at Frazier's package store at the right turn on the road back inland.

A pack of Camels along with a pint of the no-name gin stocked next to the cooking wine. Reinforcements. Packaged courage.

The nerves he usually calmed so readily with thinking and lake walks and logic and numbers in neat columns crept up his neck here like unkempt Boston ivy and bit down so hard no leisurely walk was going to relinquish the grip this time. So he gave into these occasional vices, which his coworkers used to jab at him.

"Enjoy some life, Truman," they would tell him when they saw his raw side begin to get ugly on the outside.

"Loose it, or it will curb you," they warned.

Truman's outward calm was disrupted, and since he towered over them, they rarely looked at him square-eyed enough to see that the undercurrent was not quite so serene. This electric current that lived in him was seriously unexamined. This sort of unease was such a rarity in his life that he'd never felt the need to examine the obvious mere interruption of his disposition.

All of it.

This home did not seem much now, as he viewed Martha's latticework and the roughhewn edges of the wooden structure that surrounded the trailer's midsection. A framework of jointed two-by-fours surrounded fading two-color aluminum and came together at the front to form a sort of gaunt-protector-turned-functional-porch of sorts.

So oddly constructed, yet somehow it made great sense to his logic.

Someone had tacked a military canvass over the porch-like protrusion, and Truman felt like somebody else standing there, viewing the residence where he had once belonged.

Camels and gin.

∅

Salome would see Master Planter just one more time after the Blues invaded.

"It's all changed now," Jinn told her one afternoon as she loaded eggs, milk, okra, squash and gourds, peppers, and melons into his bateaux for the market in Beaufort.

New president had forgiven Planter and his cousins.

Amnesty.

Taking it all back: that was the news offered.

Master Planter be coming for us or this place, not sure which.

Be ready.

Jinn was more defiant in this reproach than Salome had ever seen, and this coming from the man who had always seemed attached to Planter in the old days, like a leashed dog.

Salome herself had no idea she lived inside a black shawl in those old days—that was, until it returned to wrap her up again.

Fear.

The thought of facing the man who had given her the gift of Cypress smothered her not because she feared for her daughter but for herself.

She was not strong like the others.

Salome's method of maintaining seemed to have come from some other place, and she had learned early on to avoid wrath or conflict simply by going the other way.

Master Planter and the Blue General had both taught her to see that men like them had wants more important than hers.

It was all about taking. She wished she could have seen that back then. At least from the General, she stood on the proof that all the taking was worthwhile in the end.

Then she glanced at Cypress and remembered how her time with the master had given her something even greater.

No missionary or teacher had needed to explain how to hold on to that. What she needed now was help holding on to the acres that the Blues had promised would always be hers.

If Planter was on his way back, it was not Cypress he wanted but her carved-out parcel of old Tabby Place.

"I will," she told Jinn.

Be ready.

SIMON

When Simon was just six years old, neighbors referred to him as 'the boiler', as many had witnessed first-hand the release of a hateful vengeance that seemed too nasty for such a young boy.

Mothers learned quickly to steer their tender young ones clear of the ugliness that carried too much heat for their fragile souls to bear. Where he found those ugly words to spew on others, no one quite knew, and it shamed his mother to hear of such goings on.

How such a child knew how to singe another's soul was beyond Cypress, especially since he was a generation beyond his grandmother's papers and had never worked a field 'cept her own. He lived in a fortunate day where even papers were no longer required, and he wandered from house to school house to church as he willed. If only he knew what it meant to be head down and hidden in view.

He was to become her greatest life challenge, this lost boy, since Jinn had passed by then—not that he'd been much help anyhow.

Times remained hard.

Simon's discontent grew with a defiance she had not expected, and she prayed he would become more like Truman.

Quiet.

Obedient.

Respectful.

All things Salome had taught her to ignore; she had shaken her hand hard the day she'd passed on, and in spite of the fever and fatigue from her bed, she'd railed at her daughter.

Be heard!

Make noise!

Hang on!

Yet here was Cypress favoring her quiet boy, cursing the one ready to break out of all Jinn had held in.

Held in till it killed him.

Ø

The Beaufort County Courthouse burned down in 1935 and with it, the island's recorded history of land proffering, acquisition, relinquishing, desisting, and repurchasing.

Land given and taken.

Procured and then threatened with loss again.

Bought in a swindle.

Or taken.

Martha had never trusted courthouses, banks, or lawyers anyhow, so an original copy of the deed was kept under the floor inside an old lead-lined insert, covered with dank, roughhewn linoleum that had a rutted notch from the leaning back leg of Martha's kitchen chair over the years.

Truman had noticed the crevice in the floor when he'd first scanned the kitchen.

Details were his deal.

Just what is necessary, Martha decided then and there. She knew she could trust him again when he didn't ask about the obvious dent.

Safe and sound was how Martha preferred to live, and there was no better moment than that first sip of black, bitter coffee at dawn as she shifted her weight on that back right leg and dug it into her memory.

No one was taking this place from Cypress, or Martha for that matter, ever again.

She would see to that. Her turn now.

Her turn.

Negro Law of South Carolina
Slaves, Their Civil Rights, Liabilities, and Disabilities
DeBow's Commercial Review

SEC. 1. In a previous part of this digest, I have had occasion incidentally to state the meaning of the civil law maxim, *"partus sequitur ventrem,"* and of the provision of the 1st section of the Act of 1740, "the offspring to follow the condition of the mother". Both mean that the offspring of a slave mother must also be a slave.

SEC. 2. The maxim, as well as the provision of the Act, has further meaning in relation to property. It determines to whom the issue belongs. The owner of the mother has the same right to her issue born while she belongs to him that he has to her. If, for example, the person in possession is tenant for life, then such an one takes estate for life in the issue. If there be a vested estate, in remainder, or one which takes effect on the termination of the life estate, the remainder man is entitled to the issue, on the falling in of the life estate, as he is entitled to the mother. If there be no estate carved out beyond the life estate, then as the mother reverts, so also does the issue.

The first night Salome tried to walk away from Tabby Place, it was all a show, for Missus Planter even more than Master. It was in the days when she'd known for certain Master Planter would not lay a hand on his precious house girl. It was a foolish display, really: she walked out in the middle of the day, almost noon, at high tide, when no plotting soul would ever think of such imprudence.

Of course, they would have sorely paid for it, and Salome was oblivious to the consequences back then.

She saw them. Touched them.

Watched them.

And those consequences included cleaning up Bags Joe that time he almost made it, holding onto the roped side of a skiff bound for the republic, land in sight. Bags Joe didn't even make it back to the island alive, and Salome helped ol Granny clean him up as best they could before he was wrapped and dumped into the old water's edge graveyard.

Least Joe got a resting place, some said, but they'd known his was a spirit that would always roam, no matter what they left on his quick-dug grave.

They barely left him a stone-scratched cross in the dirt, the burial happened so fast, and later someone added a banded-stick cross and the rope they had found clutched in his broken hands when they'd thumped his breath out.

After that, Salome aimed for a put-on an air of reproach, as if she were the house Missus instead of the reverse. Dared to even puff it out high in her chest.

Chin up.

So young and foolish to throw out such waves of defiance, but Salome wore it like a breastplate and pushed bounds the wiser ones knew should never be breached.

Such gall, even for a kitchen servant!

No master was ever so infatuated with a house girl that he would let her cross such lines and then go about bathing his missus in flaunted apathy toward her orders.

Ol Granny knew so, but there was no convincing a pig-head like Salome of anything in those days.

Her head was lost to all she had seen, and she had not seen much.

Yet oddly enough to all of the rest, Missus Planter ignored her, and once Salome recognized what she already well knew, there was no leaving.

Not today.

Not ever.

She cowed her shoulders inward then, when the limits of her circumstance were at last seen with her own eyes, and she plodded her way back to the kitchen house, working fast to catch up on all she had missed. If she had ever thought she would get a kindly word of understanding, she knew better then. She had lost her fit with the others at that point and knew she had better get back and keep to herself the private duty with Master Planter.

It would get her nowhere to use it as a defense.

Useless and charmless.

Her mistake was letting that seep inside her and begin to rinse out all the runner self-talk. It was some time after that the babies started coming and leaving. Not grown and sold, that heart wrench for others, but never even having breathed life.

Three times.

Cypress had tried to come through at least three times before she finally took hold and held on.

The other times babies had come and gone, it had happened so early on there had never been any visible sign of carrying. That fourth time, which was, of course, the last time, Cypress popped her tummy right through her heaviest gathers early on, and Missus Planter knew there was no beating it out of her this time.

This one was staying put whether she liked it or not—and she definitely did not—but a lady would never have said. Missus Planter was a plantation daughter of the best sort, unlike her Edisto cousins, and had always held her words to the highest level, knowing better than to raise her own hand to chastise any of the house females.

She had others to do those dirty tasks for her when the need arose, and she would not resort to such filth.

Above it.

That starless night, Salome up and ran again with her muslin bag of misgivings; she thought she could save her baby. She did not know yet that Cypress was coming to save her and the others.

Yet Salome was different by then, not really listening, and there was no room for arrogance when a woman protected the one thing that was hers alone. But Master Planter reminded her it would never be hers after all—it was his.

That's when she ran again.

She understood the tides by then, too, and her own cycles that had brought a rhythm to her life even before Cypress came.

There were no little souls lost when she cried each time over the blood and painful scraps of innards and such. Ol Granny consoled her, her body wracked with sobs that were never for the loss of any child but a release from a torment that she'd never understood, and she would pass on through with the loss from yet another affliction put upon her.

Salome never once thought about ol Granny's suffering or that of the rest of them. It was always her own pain that mattered most. She was selfish like that.

If a message had been shared earlier, Salome had not heard it with her shut-up ears, and only when it was forced upon her did she wake up and recognize that the moon, the trees, the marsh, and the beach were all listening.

Waiting.

Speaking.

Cypress.

When Salome began to wait in silence with them, she finally heard those things she would later explain to her child, the things they said in the dark.

Those silent things that rocked her to sleep when sleep would not come.

It would always come now.

Words came easier, and the old prescience returned. It took less of a hold this time as Salome learned to guide it again, direct it, and focus on what was to come.

The future was all that there really was anyway.

Today was futile.

It was tomorrow that brought Cypress, and it was tomorrow that would bring her home. Where this hope arose from, she really did not know, but she had a sense of the passing and the returning from the silence around her that came through especially at dawn or in those quiet moments of post-moonlight.

Especially those walks when she was left alone by Master Planter and that could use for herself and her own thinking forward. The others did not understand this looking forward, especially ol Granny, who constantly berated her, telling her to keep her nose pointed to the ground.

"It's where you find the least trouble, and where trouble naught finds its way to you," she always said.

There was no need to leave now.

No need to run.

It was not elsewhere that she would find the safe hold for Cypress. Better would be here soon; she felt it in her bones.

Cypress was her focus then, and once better came, it would all change, and Missus Planter would matter no longer.

Cypress foretold it.

She would be ready.

Salome had never been more ready.

∅

The Blues had been at Tabby Place for more than a year when it was decided at the eve of the new year to assemble near the ancient cypress for a reading one evening.

Jinn and Salome and Cypress joined the Blues and others so gaily dressed to hear the statement that answered so many of the questions Salome had begun to ask Teacher.

Many came solely for the food and were struck by the throng of ships that had begun to approach the harbor.

Perhaps it was all more significant than it first had seemed when the invitations had gone 'round the island.

The president's proclamation was read aloud by a former statesman who had freed his own early on. He read it with such care, as if it were the president himself articulating those soft words that the Blues at first thought had fallen deaf on Jinn and the others.

Promises made.

Promises kept were entirely another matter.

Ø

There was a quiet time after Truman and Simon ran north, and Martha went on to raise her crops and her prayers in silence.

She lived on the only way she knew how, repairing and restoring Salome's cabin, plank by plank, like her mother had taught her.

Martha chased out the cold and kept it warm for her husband, Kenneth, who had been too old for the Great War and was not needed in the next, so she stuck it out with no reprieve or military payments like the families of other soldiers who returned and awaited the monthlies.

Instead she persisted alone, with a garden, a cow, two pigs, and three chickens, and plenty of room on the forty-eight acres still hers. She sold her field crops at market and even shipped some to Savannah.

It was all more than enough. Subsistence.

∅

Salome died intestate, the meaning of which Martha would only come to learn much much later, and Cypress had painted the cabin haint blue to keep her out of it.

It was not that she did not want her mother around. In fact, she most certainly felt her everywhere, but this was her cabin now, and at sixteen years, she felt like she should make it her own.

Blue to comfort her.

Symbolic of her mother's passing and of the men who had released them both.

Freed her. Cypress had been born free.

Still, night remained the hardest. Alone.

Cypress's acres were unlike the communities on the other end of the island, where land parcels were sided by similar and soulful talk well into the night.

Parcels that prayed houses and schools.

Church.

Community.

Here she was, surrounded by Master Planter's rescinded acres on one side, ocean on another, marshland on the third. She worked her own forty, but the land beyond that was sharecropped or labored on by others from Mitchelville, who went on home for their evenings.

Transients on her end of the island.

It wasn't till the following spring that Jinn, still subsisting in the seed barn, rapped at her door in that old way again, calling on a daughter, alone, who had her meals with him just like her mother had done.

Now just the two of them.

Not quite right, Teacher told her.

Impressions, Teacher had said another day, with a bit too much of the edges of Missus Planter's instruction that Salome used to mock for her.

Let them talk, Cypress responded more than once.

Census of 1860.

No.	States.	Free Population.	Slave Population.	Total.	Per Centage of Slaves.
1	South Carolina	301,271	402,541	703,812	57.2
2	Mississippi	354,700	436,696	791,396	55.1
3	Louisiana	376,280	333,010	709,290	47.0
4	Alabama	529,164	435,132	964,296	45.1
5	Florida	78,686	61,753	140,439	13.9
6	Georgia	595,097	462,232	1,057,329	43.7
7	North Carolina	661,586	331,081	992,667	33.4
8	Virginia	1,105,192	490,887	1,596,079	30.7
9	Texas	421,750	180,682	602,432	30.0
10	Arkansas	324,323	111,104	435,427	25.5
11	Tennessee	834,063	275,784	1,109,847	24.8
12	Kentucky	930,223	225,490	1,155,713	19.5
13	Maryland	599,846	87,188	687,034	12.7
14	Missouri	1,067,352	114,965	1,182,317	9.7
15	Delaware	110,420	1,798	712,218	1.6
		8,289,953	3,950,343	12,240,296	32.2

Salome had not farmed at first, as the Blues took the cotton behind her cabin, but they had walked out a perimeter for her that also closed in the seed barn. Jinn had stayed onsite, and the old Quartermaster had been certain more cotton would be planted for the treasury.

The freed would help to secure it and remain in servitude for home and board.

No doubt.

The Quartermaster had overlooked femininity for color and assigned her to the one superintendent who would be complicit in such special relief decisions made by those up north when challenged about a female head of household.

In war, all was fair.

Fair enough.

Salome had already laid the garden close up to its walls. Rations of hominy, vinegar, salt, and the like were delivered as well, along with a certain amount of wages earned for meals and baked goods delivered out of the kitchen house to support ol Granny, who had been allowed to remain as well.

What a clan they made: Jinn, ol Granny, Salome, and Cypress.

All still at home on Tabby Place.

They would surely get along.

Dare not think on Master Planter now.

Ø

Cypress had remained proud and told Martha so one visitation, which of course was not to be the last.

The cabin lasted till the dry rot took it down in '55, and Martha was forced to replace it when you could get an eight-foot-wide aluminum on contract with a mobile home title loan.

An actual home.

"Easiest money ever gotten," Kenneth bragged, pocketing ten-dollar bills from the Beaufort home lenders for every islander he'd sent up their way.

Easy money.

No buy-for loans was all he had to say.

Drive it in. Set up in less than a day.

Kenneth never mentioned the matters of septic and water and the like. Let them figure that out for themselves.

Don't messy the financing, the lenders warned him.

Sort that piece out later.

Technically, the old Tabby Place section was still all of theirs, still belonged to all heirs of Salome, but Martha's brothers would likely never again set foot there, so she used it for collateral and burned the cabin remains outside her new home throughout the winter of '56. Some resented the manufactured home.

Eyesore.

Others speculated it would be driven out for nonpayment as easily as it had been driven in, if Kenneth had his hands in it.

∅

It had been like a cleansing.

Much of the old Tabby Place plantation house had burned, but tabby itself could never burn nor rot and would remain standing. Like the old Sheldon church, burned by the Brits in the first ugly war.

The fire had not been started by the General like so many of the others but by one of the departing Blue soldiers, who had lit cinder for a smoke and flicked it, still burning, into the dry pile of leaves on the east porch.

The unnoted blaze had grown swiftly into the house, as by then the soldiers had already fled for their departing ship, the Quartermaster had gone up north for a report to the congress.

Fortunately, no one had been in the house as it burned, but the closest buildings, which were Salome's cabin and the old seed barn, were heat-burned on the sides nearest the big house.

The neighbors had rushed in too late to the site to save the big house, but they'd ensured that Salome's survived and protected the old seed barn from the flame. After the burn, those shanties were the only pieces of Tabby Place left standing, and the volunteer brigade had to see to it no more disasters struck them.

∅

Cypress was four years old when she recognized her name was the tree that would protect her.

A constant guardian that would not abandon nor exploit her. Upright gently nearby.

Patient and unfaltering. Solid and true.

Salome had repeated ol Conjur's incantation—without all the shrills and shakes, of course—and taken her to the soul-bound cypress at the marsh side of Tabby Place, the shells and skins at the shrine base where they all still placed their gifts and watched libations seep into the roots.

Someone had placed a bottle tree nearby as an extra assurance—likely after the Blues had come and left, as no one would have dared do such in the days when the Planters were here. An array of gifts had been stuck in the soggy ground, with the glassy, wide-open eyes of blue-bottoms jutting out from every stick and limb that sucked a bottle lip.

No spirits dared roam this place. It was time for them to move on anyhow.

The old days were gone, and there were no more souls to lure.

The bee's mead had gone first and was followed by the palm oil and pomegranates, food of the gods of the tree and all the old souls of this place where Salome had seen her first discontent and fought the minds of those who had impelled their will onto hers.

Shamed her for carrying Master Planter's seed and loving it as her own with no desire or attempt to rid herself of it. She'd kept at it and had not run from Missus Planter as she'd thought she might but stayed right and on her tasks from then on. She looked down at her child and tried hard to imagine how she'd lived then compared with now.

∅

The second night after Truman came back, Martha slept so deep, she dreamed for the first time she could recall.

First time in a long, long time.

It was a deep, vivid dream where she visited the daughters of Zelophehad, and, honest to God, when she awoke, she reflected for a moment on the paisley curtains, in which the only color was a brilliant orange that had survived the sun's ability to squelch the cotton frocks put upon the world.

Faded but resilient in part.

Sort of like Martha still clinching her strong will.

Single-minded, they used to call her. Not a compliment exactly, but as a girl, she had taken it as such. At least it had referred to her mental capabilities rather than her domestic skills. And she had both, actually, which was still expected for a girl.

She arose slowly, tenderly, putting her good leg down first, followed ever so gently by the other, then stood to lean toward her rough and tattered King James Bible on the upright chest, already laid open to Numbers 36.

This was the very same bible the kindly Boston abolitionist had first placed in Salome's hands for her child, and the woman had later taught Cypress to read from it.

Martha relished this particular piece of her family's history over many others mainly because it was the book that helped her see Cypress through to a life different from Salome's, even though Martha had rarely agreed with much else in it.

Simple as that. Abandoned yet never looked back.

Look forward.

Ahead is all there is.

Sometimes it was a fitting equivalent to the paradox: this biblical story of Zelophehad's daughters might as well have been her own. Been herself, more like.

Been Cypress, had it not been for Salome. Been Jinn, had it not been for Cypress.

"Over my dead body," Martha muttered quietly, and began to prepare for the new day where she was no longer in this fight alone.

At least Truman had come home.

∅

The Attorney pondered what she had just seen.

Since the goddamn first bloody year of the war.

The Attorney was astounded.

If only she had someone to tell. It had fallen in her lap as if she alone was the one to guide this unassuming woman to hang on. It was the case she had waited for, the one that might actually make all the unsaved worthwhile. One continuous lineage back to the Blues for a parcel that bordered the largest development to date on the island.

You will come to understand, was all the Attorney had said to Martha that first day.

They both had so much to tell, and it was going to take time. Time was now at a premium if she was to help this heir hang on to something far greater than property assessment and tax valuation.

It was all so very complex and yet so very simple.

You will come to understand.

I already understand, Martha had countered.

This land is all of ours. This land is us.

This land is family.

Stay put.

∅

They beat Salome heartlessly after she tried to run that first time, precious muslin in hand as the bogs sucked at her feet, and barely alive after a treacherous delivery of that first little soul to save her and the others who had not made it. She would never give up.

She cried out when she should have kept silent—it wouldn't have lasted so long—but she had the warnings so loud in her head by then, and the deep, guttural sounds from the old place left her heedless. All that was gone now.

Cypress was here and hers, as much as the voices were hers and would always be hanging over her head and taking it by whip by crick by time.

Beat it out of her.

That was their answer to any odd moment of powershift, movements only temporary but never the mind's eye. She would see the future as long as she lived, and she saw it stretch on well beyond the days of Cypress's own first child. Right here. Same place.

Prescience did little when words and slaps kept her grounded and humbled as dirt. Had never given her a future before Cypress.

Foresight had meant little when the only way through had been staying in the real as it happened.

The Blues took up Master Planter's home as their own and ordered his captors as if they were the same as the sworn-in ranks of Blue that pervaded the island.

Cypress had been and would be the only good thing she had ever done. The Blues made sure of that. She had sought comfort there, and fool's gold. Nothing was real, and no peace ever came of it. Only Cypress.

She cried the first time when they helped her to take Planter for her child. Her tears were not over lost safety, for you cannot cry over what never was. The tears were her disgust over a name not hers, not theirs.

How odd to be considered a name tied to this place where she had borne her.

Cypress Planter.

A name of time and place, even ownership, especially in this place she knew she would never leave.

A woman with a name had a chance here now.

A woman with acres of cotton had an even greater chance at something.

They came for us but mainly cotton, she explained to Cypress when she was old enough to listen, still too young to understand how it was then compared with now. Maybe she'd never know, really.

The Blues had seen to that.

Salome would see to it now and leave it to Cypress after that.

Everything from that first night on was only for Cypress. All that mattered.

∅

Truman was no activist or rights worker and was most certainly not political.

Never had been. Just wasn't in him.

Surely, he'd had the opportunity but had never taken it up. Just because he lived in turbulent times, North or South, did not mean he had joined in. He was as simple in his life as they come, and when his friends—the few friends he'd had begun their talk of religion, politics, the war, and everything else beyond the weather, really, it just made him so uncomfortable that he always found some excuse to depart or shut down.

Although some might have called him a complex thinker, others just found him quiet, simple, with a daily existence even simpler. He liked it that way.

Settled.

Predictable.

Truman liked the straightforwardness of his daily life, and whatever might brew below was best kept there where it had always been. No mess, no disruption.

In coming here to this place now so foreign to him, unlike the home far north where he'd chosen to run, he was already finding both mess and disruption. It was becoming more and more difficult to keep it all where it was.

Where it had been all this time.

Unsettled but under control.

This current was now running through Truman, and he wondered whether he would ever find a way to wrap it all up again the way it had been when he'd left this place.

Wrapped up.

Buttoned up.

Tightly bound.

Yet here in this climate, he needed the current. He needed the rising tide, and for the first time, he let it engulf him. Inward to out.

In the two short days since Martha's call, the unraveling had begun.

Truman was no rabble-rouser, and yet this lawyer had stirred something in him. Something deep and raw that he somehow knew had always been there.

Turbulence.

A deep current moved within him now, and Truman dared not recognize or even acknowledge it. Truman had hung up the phone after Martha filled him in, and all the old days had come out of the places he'd thought he had hid them so well.

Unsettled.

∅

The Captain's son didn't quit the trade until the illegal trade stopped him. Even after, cargo was cargo, and found short runs were best.

His routes were easier than the old Middle Passage, where too many deaths riddled the voyage, and now many ready brokers and buyers served direct to plantation owners.

The ship that had brought Salome was long past the trade embargo. Years past.

The vociferous Captain assured Master Planter that full cotton export to the king's land would not be an empty return; however, it was one that still dallied in the wrong places to capture easy prey like infants and old women over sturdy field hands. But it had brought him Salome and ol Granny, and for that, he was grateful.

That same year, the Captain saw the greatest ever investment in these round trips. Not our congress, Master agreed, complicit in the illegal after-trade ensued till the Blues arrived.

When Master Planter's cousins heard the Captain was caught with captives aboard that last time, they watched in suspicion as he shook his head while the story was shared, feigned shock at any who would accept such malevolent traffic, as if his own hands were clean of such trade.

Groom skill at home had been his directive, though the cousins knew full well he would look away during any such barter. Or worse.

Had always lived too close to the edges, they said.

∅

Martha planned to be buried next to Cypress at the water's edge graveyard, where Cypress had picked herself out a plot just before she'd become ill.

Or perhaps it was her prescience.

The hour of her waterside service, a great crane had lifted from the green water just moments after Martha had dropped a rose into the burial plot.

Or perhaps simultaneous.

Respect.

Cypress's spirit was quiet as night for days after.

∅

That second time Salome held on to her acres, she knew she held a possessory title and it would be enough.

Pre-emption. Just knew it.

The Quartermaster who'd favored her had advised her well.

Hang on. Stay put.

Head of family. Now she knew those words, too. Legal status.

Salome had farmed her own acres since the Blues had departed. She'd never left and had kept up her own place best she could, even better than most, thanks to Jinn. She'd even planted her own cotton, which some of her neighbors had steered clear of, entirely unsure of how to proceed without the old way.

The challenge was no surprise when the superintendent told her it was coming. Two tracts, twenty acres each, not one, like she'd originally been told.

Possessory was another word she had learned to spell, and her teacher applauded as she expounded her rights as property owner.

Salome even let out a piglet-squeal, and Cypress laughed with her.

Yet no education had prepared her for the familiar rap at the door by a stooped-over, tattered old man and a much younger version in more recent finery.

Get off our land by end of the month, the younger Planter ordered, and the old man Planter just stood and stared at her from the back, scanning the cabin background for a glimpse of Cypress, who had no need to hide.

Paid the taxes and coming back for it.

Amnesty.

The younger spewed the meager words that he meant to be solid, but they failed to resonate with this oily-head-scarfed woman he had always viewed as invisible. Junior was only here for Senior, who had lost his old self in a war he had once actually urged.

Petitioned. The pitched battle would not take long.

∅

"Cypress born free, you know."

Martha's declaration startled Truman from his focus on the island-long drive from ocean to marsh to causeway to the interior route to the courthouse.

The causeway was a colossal structure that angled around to connect inland and had him reflecting on his father, childhood, and the patience he and Martha had had when the structure did not exist. This path to the North had not even existed when Truman had somehow finally found a way to leave the island.

Simply put down his hoe and said that's that, then.

Whether it had been a conflict with Kenneth or the cotton failure had pushed him, Truman finally decided there must be something other than just plant-silk to turn a dollar.

"It's a glorious day to be alive," Truman had said every single morning of his childhood. Martha doubted he still did.

"You can't know history until it is repeated," Truman reminded Martha long after she'd expected a response.

Just an ignorant old man who needed reminding. Martha kept the thought to herself.

No need for more brother trouble now.

∅

Like a doctor who must tell you the worst case he has seen in order to prepare you for the bad news regarding your own disorder, the Attorney told Martha and Truman about the worst partition inequity she had ever encountered.

It could be worse, she began.

A freedman had thirteen children, twenty-four grandchildren, eighteen great-grandchildren, she began. *Almost all had lived on a twenty-acre tract since the war ended.*

The freedman had lived to be 102 and, as is most often the case, had left no will. It had been a puzzle of freedmen's cabins amid manufactured homes brought in every which way as the children had grown, married, had children, grown, married, had children.

A multi-generational homeplace.

Three of the children had died and never married, so grandchildren as they grew up and married moved into the houses as the deceased vacated them.

This family had grown over decades.

Lived their whole lives on those twenty acres.

No pursuit of wealth.

Subsistence.

Countenance.

It's a privilege to stay put, the grandmother had instructed, until she'd passed on and a great-grandchild had moved into the first freedman shanty—his great-grandfather's—still standing at the center.

So far, this was a familiar story to Martha.

She knew many island families like this, especially of late, and knew many who had been forced out, but never with so many layers, so she was curious as the Attorney went on.

There was no way to measure in inches or feet where one heir's portion began or another's ended, the Attorney continued.

It had been a cramped but shared community, and they had believed it would continue like that forever, until one of the grandchildren had married a woman from Beaufort and moved off the island.

That was where the Developer's people had found him, and his new wife's family had convinced him to sell his interest for cash. *He no longer lived there, so why not line his pocket for his own children,* the Attorney rationalized in the retelling.

Cash in the bank.

The grandson had been paid five hundred dollars cash, the Attorney said and moved in on the clincher.

Five hundred dollars cash, Martha repeated, as she knew what was to come. She had witnessed enough departing families moving off their land only to watch as a hurricane-proofed monstrosity replaced them.

The resort charges five hundred dollars per night, the Attorney said, as if that would get a reaction from Martha.

Must be oceanside, Martha responded.

They all want the water now.

Yes, and of course the freedman's family had had no resources to fight the partition suit. They all were evicted with nowhere to go.

Had lost their land in an ugly exploitation that had left generations homeless, except the grandson and his family in Beaufort, of course.

Destitute. A legacy of loss.

Trouble. Alcohol. Drugs. Suicide. Jail. You name it.

Predictable, the Attorney said.

Martha counted on one hand the heirs with interest in her parcel: Martha, Truman, and Simon. Hers just could not be as difficult as all that.

Stay put.

∅

"The cloudy status of the title has probably helped Martha to hold on to this for the past thirty years, but no longer," the Attorney continued.

Another heir.

Not her brothers. Not Martha.

"Simon has a daughter," she continued. Martha and Truman dropped jaw. "One Jolene Tyre. Apparently, Simon had a daughter in 1960 with Helena of the Daufuskie Tyres."

"A daughter," Martha echoed. "A niece."

The Attorney asked carefully, "Where is Simon?"

"Your guess is better than mine," Martha replied.

"Well, Miss Tyre—who by the way now strategically goes by Jolene Tyre Planter," the Attorney continued. "Ms. Tyre Planter has sold her interest in the parcel to the Sea Island Development Company to force a partition sale. Very likely, she has been given cash and legal representation to bring this forward."

Seen it too often.

"How do we know if she is truly Simon's daughter?" Martha ventured.

"We find Simon. You have Truman here already, so all heirs are represented except for Simon. We need Simon to dispute this alleged daughter's paternity so that we can make her claim as Simon's heir, well, suspect," the Attorney explained.

"And if she is his daughter: what then?" Martha countered.

"We must meet her, know her first. You must understand that this woman is not on your side."

Visibly frustrated, the Attorney had a new edge to her voice. Truman sensed this was the simplest and cleanest family tree she had yet encountered.

Martha slid forward the weathered, government-issue document full of nineteenth-century calligraphy bearing Salome Planter's name. Clean lines from human ownership to land ownership—lost twice and retrieved. A singular forty-eight acres of heirs' property retained by consecutive heirs since the first year of the war.

"Decades of holding on," the Attorney said, letting out a slow whistle as she touched the parchment. "More than a century, really. A new era with a new war."

The Attorney was always buoyed by new heirs' battles. The Sea Island Development Company.

No more edge in her voice now.

∅

Cypress stood all of her four-years-tall, proud, and filled up like a mid-floor fountain. She knew it right then, full well, that Master Planter's glance could disarm her mother, and she would not have it. She saw it. She felt it.

Without an uttered sound from Cypress, Salome pulled her chin straight up off her chest and glared at both men with a silent, steely-eyed stare so fierce they actually stepped back from the doorway.

"Let her be," Master Planter said to Junior. "Let her be."

But Salome did not have long after that promise, and she sought out the agent in Mitchelville with her teacher's help.

If only that was to be the last time, the last challenge.

Hang on. Stay put.

In Mitchelville, plans for repurchase of the freedmen's bequests had been underway since the amnesty had pillaged the General's orders, and Salome arrived in time to buy it all back, the forty tillable now surveyed at forty-eight total acres with outbuildings, and the abolitionist helped put up the $1.25 for each one that saved Salome's title.

The deed was successfully recorded.

Fifty cents up front. Seventy-five cents with deed recorded.

"You were one of the clever ones." The agent looked down at mother and child shadowed by Jinn, who stood as backdrop. "You stayed put. So many were lost and confused about where to reside, but you stayed put. Right where you needed to be."

As if there had been anywhere else to go, Salome thought as she looked down at Cypress and then back at Jinn.

Eventually, Junior finished with law school and reacquired almost all of the original fifteen hundred acres of old Tabby Place for Senior's redemption, excepting the lone forty-eight acres in the singular named deed of one Salome Planter.

Freewoman. Head of household.

Landowner.

Sea Island Cotton: Its culture, improvement, and diseases
W.A. Orton, 1912

Without seed selection, Sea Island Cotton cannot be grown successfully for more than a few years in any latitude. The interior growers have always depended on the skillful seed selection of the Carolina planters and have continued to neglect the matter since this seed supply was cut off by a growers' organization. No more improved seed can be had from the Sea Islands, and nothing is more certain than that the crop will continue to deteriorate rapidly until the interior growers begin work to improve it. They will undoubtedly rise to the occasion when they realize their industry is at stake. They may be assured in advance that they will succeed to a degree limited only by the care and skill they expend.

It was somewhere around 1850 when the anonymous letter arrived at the South Carolina Legislature's Committee on Sea Island Cotton.

At the same time the letter landed on a desk in Columbia, it was rumored in of the cotton exchange that some inimitable round bales stamped *Planter* were not only garnering an unheard ask of $1 per pound but that *pre-orders* had actually begun arriving from across the pond. Pre-orders for the extra-long staple, now sometimes called ELS, were something else altogether, as they were *pre-paid* pre-orders at $1.01.

Even if these stories seemed far-fetched, this shook the greedy hearts and souls of the Seabrooks, the Baynards, the Edings and Ephraims and Master Planter's other coastal cousins.

"Just what is his secret?"

The cousins would cajole one another just in case the other knew something they did not.

All of this, of course, was no secret to the Liverpool buyers, who had known for some time that Master Planter's luxurious ELS was quite different and was awarded its own acronym to further set it apart from other more general forms of Sea Island Cotton. Their best spinners had told them so, and no other island planter had offered a match to the superiority of Planter's cultivar.

Later some would say Master Planter had likely penned this letter himself and had intended it to feed the frenzy surrounding his planting secrets on a political scale in readiness for the cultivation of his own personal agenda.

Cotton money brought power not only to the South but to the North as well, where the economy had come to rely on this flow of currency. He was certainly owed a seat at the table at the secession convention or even more once South Carolina was sovereign. After all, it had been his blood that had carved out these acres over a hundred years prior, brought in the first field hands to lay in rice and indigo, and found fortune on a previously treacherous stretch of coastline inhabited by the uncivilized.

Yes, it was his blood right.

For now, Master Planter enjoyed the attention from a distance, as well as the pining jealousy of his Edisto and James Island cousins up and down the seaboard. He lauded his goldmine and enjoyed their painful reactions a bit too much. Yet the irony was not lost on them that his plantations on their islands did not produce dollar-cotton; it was only the bales from Tabby Place that took home the ask they coveted for themselves and set the precedent to which they all aspired.

They all knew well before this that cotton grown on the island was different somehow, so when his cousins ventured to Tabby Place—where Master Planter now spent the majority of his time—and beg for seed and perhaps a glimpse of this wondrous variety, he smiled his broadest, most generous smile and said, "Oh *surely*."

"Help yourself in the seed barn," he offered, pointing to the decoy.

There they found bags and seed ready for the taking, as if they were at market. Only later, after shaking off their biased views of the avaricious cousin as they filled their seed bags, did they realized they'd been duped.

The real seed barn, of course, was Jinn's own quarters, which appeared more like a tabby barn than the usual quarter. Not even all of the cotton pickers knew this was where Jinn not only spent his days but also most of his nights.

The anonymous committee letter had goaded the entire state.

> *While the secret I am about to share would most assuredly garner a lucrative payment, out of benevolence to the greater good, I have deemed it better to share it with the public trust that your committee represents.*
>
> *The state should explore the effects of salt marsh as fertilizer and the contiguity of cotton fields and salt rivers, for it is no coincidence that cotton grown on Sea Island is vastly superior to the upland long-staple sort. The boon to the state economy cannot be predicted if all were to follow this technique.*

Master Planter had no need to sign the letter, as he had already taken the crown as his own by then. It closed with the preemptive:

> *Salt alone is the primary secret of ELS SI Cotton and the key to the cotton kingdom.*

Of course, the letter was bogus for it had left out the principle secret carried on by the old West Indies seed man.

Many would say later that Master had begun to believe his own press and had stood over Jinn for so many years that he believed that it was his own hands at work in that barn rather than those of the man he owned.

In Master's mind, Jinn was simply a tool, like a sifter or a rake. For he owned Jinn just as much as he owned an inanimate five-tine manure fork that pitched the salt marsh fertilizer onto a new crop in his isolated empire, a mere physical extension of his own arms and mind.

Jinn was his, bought and paid for, so of course he knew that in spite of all the gadgetry—saw versus roller gins, and the new science of the plant cycle—Jinn's gift was his hands, and finger-ginning *after* moting was the real secret to ELS: the vital secret he would never share with anyone else.

I possess Jinn's hands as much as a garden trowel or fork or any other planting device in my vast inventory, Master Planter convinced himself again and again.

Not a man. Not hands, but tools.

Paper to prove it.

Yet in the deepest of sleep, Master Planter's mind pitched and rolled with this rationale and left him burdened till dawn. His only relief was from the can-see dawn to the can't-see dusk, when he stood over Jinn's hands at the tabby barn seed bench and watched them at work. There he found a beauty that melted away all those slumbering doubts of whose seed whose.

So it was that in those days, Master Planter did little else, and Jinn, of course, had no choice but do the same.

⌀

As Martha told Jolene about the years of weevil and cotton destruction, Jolene understood well it was a better explanation of her father than she had ever previously heard.

The 1919 shredded crop had been the last straw for Simon, but Truman, of course, had been more formal about his plan of departure. He had not been one prone to haste and impulsive action, but when it came to weevils, even Truman had had no choice by 1920.

Neither would stay and become what they watched happen with the others.

Beaten again.

"Truman was not one to be beat down," Martha said, and Jolene nodded. "Weevil destroyed men's innards in a way that previously only women could do."

Jolene nodded from brief experiences with men though Martha knew it would never get in the same as those who lived it.

"Poor Simon was beaten before he even got up to bat. That was just who he was, and Cypress always said it was because of Jinn. Simon carried all of it in his belly and sought whatever means there was to cool it down. Just like his father.

"Too much alike, those two was," Martha said, repeating a lifelong Cypress lecture. "It wasn't just the cotton plant gone. It slowly but surely devoured a man's soul as it left."

∅

Perhaps if the parcel had been way out in the back, out of sight of the big house, Master Planter may not have yearned for the seed barn; seeing Salome among his greatest work was more than he could bear.

Salome's acres were a new center for Tabby Place, always true north of the burned-out big house, and had even roped in his seed barn and all the remnants of a cotton glory.

Neighbors not caretakers.

Owners not tenants.

The nonpossessory Tabby Place freedmen, lost and confused over a records mess of inaccurate titles, unfiled deeds, and what to do with certificates the Blues had handed them, had lost their places through no fault of their own.

Displaced. Dispossessed. Transient.

So what else to do?

What was always done: biting the next carrot, heading out for those 80-acre inland plots handed out as homesteads, and leading their families to Alabama, Mississippi, even as far in as Arkansas.

They arrived to find non-tillable tracts of junked-out sand that no self-respecting field-hand-turned-farmer would have bought outright and had to sharecrop the neighbors' good soil.

Tenancy. Destitute.

So it went in this altered South when Master Planter left all of old Tabby Place to the son, who left it to the grandson, and by 1930, no member of the Planter family—save Salome of course—ever wanted to set foot on the island. Because of this, the grandson ended up selling the rest of it to the timber partners who bought up plots around the handful of island freedmen with solid land titles for what he hoped would be good use of failed plantations.

By then, it was Cypress's full turn to hold on.

Stay put.

⊘

In three short days, Martha had grown again on Truman, like it had been between them in the old days, and he felt a connection he would not again abandon. At least not while he was here and in her presence.

A witness to her sheer grit. Reminded him of Cypress, but would never tell her such.

Perhaps it was more that the island was the past as well as the present—trapped in time. *Compressed.*

Perhaps just setting foot again on this island clouded one's perception of the present, and in one quick turn, the scenery might change—or perhaps never had—and he'd stepped back 120 years and touched the beginning of the family.

The past seemed deeper than future, and here he had no need to scuttle the surface.

Perhaps even more importantly, it was here where he fit better. *Settled.*

∅

Salome was no longer a young girl when Master Planter came back that first time after the new president gave in his first reclamation order. She had learned enough by then from the Blues and the teachers to keep her head about her and not be swayed by the old talk and fear-mongering over tax relief and property retrieval.

She would hold fast to what she had been given by all of them.

Salome first saw Master Planter in a crumpled heap on the bottom step of the old seaside master entrance. Everyone had begun to call it Old Tabby Place by then, for it had been annihilated, stripped of its former splendor and glory, sort of like the aging grey man lying prone at its feet as though the structure was some oracle she had first read about with Miss Cleaver: the Master as an aging wise man seeking truth and finding paradox in its stead.

The hangman's knot would be too fine an escape for the man who had put more than one good soul in the ground to secure a cotton price.

She watched him fall face down on the steps of this burned-out altar to prosperity that no longer existed and actually found herself pitying him for a moment for the impossibilities he purported. Things had changed, and he would never nor could ever return to his former grandeur and fame.

Missus Planter had not accompanied him, and Salome could only imagine where she was today, having lost two sons to a war that had changed everything for both of them. Addicted to deep drinking, some reported.

But Master's son Ephraim, Jr. accompanied him. Now a grown man of seventeen years, ready to assume his father's retribution. The losses of the war had already carved out a son as a polished but sharped-edgy man.

Then Master saw her.

Salome quickly looked down out of deference for the old man's grief and former status as owner, master, and father of her child. She would not catch his eye, though she actually longed to, for doing so would allow him to have a hold once again or to 'never put asunder'— like the gospel words he had used on her to instill his ownership in the old days, as if they were man and wife, when she was only a child.

"Anathema," had been all ol Granny used to say when Salome repeated the Master's words to her at eleven then twelve, then when she'd been fifteen and carrying Cypress.

She stood out the southern boundary of the hobbled acres of cotton and vegetables that were now hers and she somehow knew he would not take them from her. If Missus Planter had been here, perhaps it would have all turned out different, but somehow he'd left her to it that day. She was never told to evacuate from her land or turned out for wage labor like the rest of the divisions of old Tabby Place marked out by the Blues.

She had done just as the General had told her to do and improved the cabins, especially the one they considered the house. She'd had no husband to suit up in blue and take off with the troops, and she had no family beyond Cypress, but somehow the Blue General had given her the forty tillable and its buildings anyhow and had never had treated her like the other refugees.

Black acres.

Only she had known the price.

Salome was surprised that Master Planter relinquished it so easily, mainly because she had the old seed barn on her side of the boundary, which had not burned. Certainly, it hadn't been maintained as it should have been all these years, but it hadn't been burned by the Blues on their departure like the big house. Jinn had been beside her watering it heavily during the big house fire to protect the barn and cabins from harm, and all of its innards had remained intact.

Now the old master would be her neighbor, and it would not take long after that for Jinn to slip over that line and back into Master's good graces.

"What would the good Lord think up next?" Salome queried the superintendent when she brought Cypress to the new white one-room school built by the missionaries on the other side of the island.

What next?

∅

By 1919, weevil had made its way up the river from Mexico, crossed the antebellum South to the island, and feasted upon the premier cotton plant in a maneuver never seen before, preferring the luxurious plants to upland and inland sorts.

Weevil had come and eaten up Sea Island Cotton like nothing they had seen. It had gorged on the larger squares and leaves but especially the bolls. It had fed on those bolls when it had touched them so little throughout the prior journey to the promise land. In less than fourteen days, one weevil had returned a man's autonomy and hopes to the wasteland of want and fear.

Burnt.

Ash.

A weevil, no larger than a water bug, had eventually destroyed the Sea Island Cotton industry in one fell swoop. Unlike their father, Jinn's sons escaped with the rest.

North.

There was nowhere else to go.

⊘

Fortunately, Jinn loved cottonseeds as much as he loved the symmetry of the thriving cotton plant.

He had the eye.

It would be decades and decades later that a genetic sequence was established for Sea Island cotton, that the word genome would be uttered by scientific minds. Much sooner for DNA and the like, but for now, Jinn simply knew in his bones that this cottonseed was different.

Somehow, he had it in his own genes to read the seeds like no other.

Kitt, the old West Indian at Bleak Hall, had told him so as a young boy, when he'd been known for selecting seeds that offered unforeseen textures, long fibers, and glorious lint. Jinn had been only a boy when he'd learned Kitt's simple arithmetic for tagging about fifty plants from each year's fields, that would later be weeded down to exactly half. Always in that collection of twenty-five, give or take, there would be one plant that would be isolated to perpetuate ELS through another crop of five hundred to propagate five more acres and a general cash crop of pure cotton wealth for the master.

Jinn had achieved a sophisticated rotation and never, ever lost track of his gold—"It's dolla' for Master," Kitt had reinforced again and again—nor inadvertently contaminated his seed treasure with other less fortuitous plants.

Dolla' meant everything to Master Planter.

By the first year at Tabby Place, Master Planter and his annual cultivars were even more pure. Distinct ELS characteristics and his discovery of the salt marsh fertilizer from the rice paddies had been an unexpected and highly-valuable find. His first motivation had been to somehow bulk up the cotton so that it was longer and heavier in its lint, so he observed the plants closest to the salt river and saw the effect on the future. When ELS became longer and finer with each cotton cycle—and more dolla'-worthy, as Kitt would have told Jinn—it finally reached the unheard ask of a dollar per pound for those tall, cylindrical bales stamped *Planter*, a name Jinn could never have known just how much he would come to despise.

Master Planter had acquired Jinn through what was purely an act of God, but it was also an event they would both ponder for years to come. For Jinn, it had been no coincidence, no godly intervention:

sheer fate had brought him to find Camorra at Tabby Place, and that was the only good reason for the relocation. The seeds were circumstantial and filled his mind with the patterns and complexities he needed, as well as helping him to avoid the harsher fieldwork for which he was unfit.

Kitt had seen early on at Bleak Hall that such a soft boy would not last long and had made Jinn his second at the seed table, thereby protecting him until the master died and his son converted to the latest in gin techniques and machinations. The old seed barn was disassembled and handwork ceased; all operations were moved to the new gin house.

Jinn thought of that last day, when the son of the Bleak Hall master had stood so prideful as the handwork was torn up and the young Jinn was left without duty.

"Old ways are done here!"

The bitter master's son had spewed his revenge on his dead father who had wasted so much time on such outmoded ideas, and glared at Jinn as if he were Kitt and complicit.

"Good riddance," he muttered as Jinn was sold for less than nothing to Master Planter on the other end of the island and transported same day to his new owner.

"Can't work the fields," he had overheard his descriptor.

"Mostly know his way round a gin house."

Soft as lint.

"Seedman," Jinn had mumbled as he met up with the overseer and to his surprise, he was sent to a corner barn built more like a cabin, hidden behind the big house at Tabby Place, and faced square up with Master Planter.

"Hear they call you finger-gin," Master Planter had greeted him.

"Jinn." He had dared to correct Master even back then.

In his best dramatic display, Master Planter swept his outstretched arm as if showing the governor himself into the parlor.

"Seed table." He gestured and enunciated as if Jinn were a child.

"Seed tray." He pointed in the same.

"Seed boy." He fingered Jinn with a sharp stab to the sternum, the hospitality having quickly dissipated, and he honed in to deliver his most critical point.

"My boy."

How Master Planter had come to know the natural talent and gifts Jinn possessed, no one was ever to learn, but spies across the island plantations were rampant, and secrets from one carried over to the next as chattel was sold and processed and traitor overseers paid off.

The price of cotton in those days often bought another price beyond the exchange of bales that made its secrets just as lucrative, and those good Christians could justify anything in the name of commerce.

Kitt's seed knowledge was to live on in Jinn when it may just as easily have been squandered, had he been sent to the field by some ignorant new owner who had no clue of his gift.

Only some greedy messenger wanting his palm lined had filled in Master Planter, and they had laughed together during that momentous exchange over the pittance paid for this seed boy, who had the eye and sheer tenacity for the pain-staking work of cottonseed finger-ginning.

Yes, the secrets uncovered in this tabby-foundered seed barn would eventually bring the death of them both.

So it was by the time Truman was four, Martha three, and Simon was walking, that Cypress found Jinn in the remains of that old tabby-base seed barn still residing out back.

Jinn was stone cold by then, eyes fixed in a stare at the floor of overturned seed trays tossed all about his slumped-over self.

She was not surprised and would not, nor could not, grieve for what was already lost.

This had been coming for quite some time. *For Jinn's sake, it could not have come any sooner*, she thought as she slowly lowered his eyelids so they were completely shut.

What she did not see until she turned back to the door, so rarely left open these days, was the observant silhouette of young Simon.

⌀

Salome had run only that once.

After that, the Blues had come and she had no need to run further. But that one time, she'd been frantic to carry her unborn across some imaginary line they had all told her about.

If she could have crossed that line before her baby came, the baby would not be owned.

She or he would have been her own.

She had stuffed the muslin bag with all she had and left Master Planter's gifts for some other to find, some other who could take her bed and accommodate his visits.

There were no visitations now anyhow.

Salome felt as big as her cabin, and loneliness ate her up inside, since Missus would not allow her in the kitchen house no longer.

Ol Granny brought her cakes and spuds and fed her after all the others had had theirs, and she always kept back an extra special thing as a surprise.

Special thing for this special baby coming, ol Granny would say.

Eat up.

That baby never saw breath, much less freedom.

CYPRESS-JINN

By 1890, the price for Sea Island Cotton had dropped to four cents, and Cypress had taken up with Jinn. Jinn had changed his last name from Planter to Seedman as a final act of defiance after leaving Master Planter that third time.

No one knew exactly why Jinn had sold himself back to Master Planter after he'd rescinded the acres Salome had been bequeathed and passed on to Cypress. It had been the first time Cypress hung on and kept her carved-out parcel as her own, left intestate in 1877. Some called it the end of a reconstruction that had been left half-built.

Cypress and Jinn had no children at first, and so many wondered why she had taken up with a man twice her age looking to suck on her youth.

It was a pastoral place with boundaries walked off early on by a Blue soldier who had never surveyed a city block, much less an acre. The barn/cabin seed house was part of this segment, and some said this was the real reason Jinn knocked on Cypress's door that first time. He longed to hand-gin his treasured seed as if it were the boon of 1860, but it was never really been the same for him without Master's praise over his shoulder, goading his sorting talent in a way that puffed Jinn out like nothing else ever could or would—not even Cypress.

Many said he was almost forty years when he sauntered back to the old Tabby Place that morning and pounded on Master's door. Jinn was tired, lonely, and hungry, the three things a former plantation seed man with a keen eye for coarse, lint-bitten trash seed could never afford if he intended to stay sharp. Ol Granny was back in the big house by then too, to care for Master. Not that she lasted long after that; at least she died in her old bed in the under room, which was all she had really wanted at the end anyhow. The shanty built just before the Blues invaded had never much suited her.

That feeling of home that had hit Jinn heavy in the gizzard when he saw ol Granny could not have been greater, and he fell to his knees and wept at her calves as if she were already dead and an indwelling haint. But no, she was still alive then, and that was all he needed for a time.

It was what sustained his desire to be somewhere he was needed or at least wanted to be.

Wanted.

Needed.

Elsewhere in those wandering in-between years, he had not found this same need or self-purpose. He had never been much of a farmer and had failed at growing anything beyond a breed plant, and harvest was certainly beyond fingers meant for seed picking over a boll.

By the 1890 census, Cypress was not even thirty years herself and yet had taken up with Jinn, by then an old man. The census worker almost put down Cypress's last name as Seedman before Jinn spoke up that it was only his. *But she had taken up with the old man, and they lived in the same house, so they were a couple if not husband-wife,* the census worker thought aloud.

Mr. Freeman down the road had taken a name common for many, but Jinn had decided to use his name to declare who he was, who he would always be. Cypress had had no choice but to continue on for her mother and father. Like it or not, she had come from both. Mixed blood without the privilege of the other. No one really knew or cared much about privilege then anyhow.

Island freedman did pretty much as they wanted then, and no one bothered them on some desolate island reachable only by ferry or bateaux.

It was the common law in those days—the first rules of some different order brought down by the North. It was still a new way of thinking about freedmen, with farms and land and acres and seed, and the legalities of marriages never wanted by owners in the before was just a part of all that new thought.

Jinn was from the old way and Cypress had been born in the new, so they never really saw eye to eye on much, since their eyes had seen it so different from the start. Yet the hanging on had only just begun then, and they were still too naïve to see that it was coming.

"Planter," she loudly corrected, and watched closely while the name was scratched out and corrected on the card.

"I am the daughter of Salome Planter. We take the mother's in this family," she instructed the worker. The surname was now properly recorded for perpetuity.

Jinn muttered something ugly that could not be heard, only felt, and headed out the door.

"He will come back for you—still thinks he own you," Jinn warned. "You think he don't, but he does. Maybe not like before, but in his own way, he will take what is his."

Always had. Always would.

"I was born free," Cypress gently reminded him, especially those days, when she treated him more like a child than her old man. "Anyhow, he way too old to come back for all this now. What would he do with it anyway?"

Cypress turned back and smiled at the census worker, embarrassed by this interchange, and ignored Jinn's raucous departure.

Jinn was a better man and still very alive when the 1900 census worker took their names again as the distinct Cypress Planter and Jinn Seedman, the common-law, childless couple who had no idea they were almost due for a short three years of domestic bliss in 1902, 1903, and 1904.

Truman came first, then Martha, then Simon, and Cypress appeared pregnant throughout all those three years in a good, fat-happy way.

Serene, they all said.

Calm.

Never seen her so settled.

Three Planter children now stood in a birth-order row: Truman, Martha, and Simon. Cypress lined them up in front of a man they had always called Jinn and would only later—much later—understand to be their father.

He had provided their seed, Cypress told them in passing one visit to the water's edge graveyard to tell the story of Salome, lest they forget as they grew older.

Cypress was enough father for them, she told them.

There was no arguing that Cypress was a force that seemed to quell any man in her path, and this reputation kept most out of any corridor she intended to follow. She had always been enough.

Cypress took care of herself. Mother-father for her children, like in the old way.

Enough. Had to be. It was all there was back then.

⌀

Martha did not really know what possessed this woman next to her, but she felt taller beside the Attorney. She cared little that she hardly knew her because she seemed to be able to lift her chin off her chest, something Martha had not done herself for quite some time. Maybe it was because she anchored her in some way or elevated her with an unspoken lift of presence. It was enough of a presence to keep the Attorney straight and tall, without rigidity, and it felt like she shared this to lift Martha up and out of herself.

Perhaps it was as simple as that.

She could be noticed now—no longer an invisible, voiceless aging woman who no one wanted to see or hear.

Voiceless.

Useless.

She now had a voice, even if it was through this Attorney. She no longer cared about the vehicle as much as her need to be heard.

It was time.

Are the property owners from 121 Blackgum Tree Road here?

Yes, sir.

Missus Planter Bailey, the family's matriarch, the Attorney introduced Martha.

Martha enjoyed hearing the word 'matriarch' and found herself mouthing it. Rolling 'matriarch' around as if it were a piece of black licorice, sucking it for all its marrow and guts. But the fear of this enrobed man stopped up any joy it might have brought her.

Martha Bailey, are you the daughter of Cypress Planter? Granddaughter of Salome Planter?

Invoking the names of Salome and Cypress was nothing short of opening the door to a chasm for which Martha was quite unprepared today.

Is the petitioner present?

No, your honor, I represent Miss Planter.

The girl had propagated Simon's name after all.

Whatever hopes she had of standing toe-to-toe with her niece were quashed. The Lawyer clearly was not from around here.

As quickly as the parties were introduced, the judge slammed a gavel and ordered the motion denied. The partition action would continue.

Martha had not uttered a word and began to slip down.

Falling.

But the Attorney would not let her fall; she grabbed Martha's arm before she had slumped six inches.

Jolene Tyre—now known as Jolene Planter—had sold her non-possessory interest to the Sea Island Development Company to force a partition action.

Three well-dressed gentlemen left the door of Courtroom #3, and Martha had no idea what this all meant, but she knew from the Attorney's face that it was not what they had wanted.

Her plea lay in her face, wordless.

"We shall certainly find out," she responded with bravado Martha wanted to believe but doubted she could. "I have no doubt we will find out."

The confidence calmed her for a moment, and she took Martha's elbow again to reinforce her words.

"May we approach the bench, your honor?" the Attorney politely queried.

As if there had not been enough surprises today. Martha turned toward the Attorney's voice.

"I represent Missus Planter in this situation." She continued to speak directly to the judge, and Martha was glad she had found her.

"Well this is interesting." The judge smiled. "I have already ruled."

"We just request a brief delay, sir. Would you please grant us an additional ten days during which Missus Planter can contact the other heirs of this property? We want them to consider their collective rights, especially since they are not all represented here today. No one seems to recognize that Simon Planter has not been located."

The Developer and his team had left just a few moments too early.

"The partition action moved ahead without full representation of all property heirs. We argue for time to allow Missus Bailey locate all heirs to this parcel. Namely Simon Planter."

Martha would not be bowed. Whether Cypress was lifting her up could only ever be speculated by those on the island who still believed in such visitations.

Granted.

Return here in one week.

The judge had four other partition actions to consider that day, all driven in some way by the Sea Island Development Company.

No harm in one extension, though the Developer would likely see it differently.

∅

Cypress's prescience was clear to all of them by the time she turned two years old.

When the first forecast manifested, it was a simple thing really, though not to Salome, who had squelched her own sight for going on eighteen years. Together they would begin to use it to protect what the Blues had given.

This quarter-quarter section of old Tabby Place had been walked off by a Blue and marked out hard and fast by none other than the Quartermaster himself, although he'd driven none of its corner stakes, instead taking her hand and leading her to the great desk to make the original bequest. The green-eyed Blue captain had stood erect at the corner of Master Planter's immense old study, which was now was the Quartermaster's.

Salome often felt this all as a dream when she replayed the events in early slumber. Drifting off to sleep, she saw herself not in her muslin but as Missus Planter in her traveling clothes descending the great front steps of Tabby Place, ordering her children to depart the hot mosquito temperatures for her summer home in Beaufort.

Yet by the time a new president had pardoned Master Planter's tax burden, opening the door to overturning his relinquishment, Salome had begun to trust her own sight again, too, and saw him coming.

Ready for him this time. His words fell away on an afternoon sea breeze as she entered the tabby kitchen cabin she had since made her own.

∅

Jinn was unsettled. Never found a place outside a gin house or seed shed.

Freedom did not really ever fit with him in the aftertime. Restless was a word they would tack on him, but it was never quite enough to describe the agitated state he remained in till that cold June when his toddler saw him dead in the corner of the seed barn that he had felt was his own despite being on Cypress's land.

The seed trays had been overturned, tossed about at random. Like he had been looking for something, not out of a willful fury.

Home Manufactures: 1. COTTON

DeBow's Commercial Review

The property engaged in growing cotton is worth $700,000,000 and the value of cotton estates is found in the negroes, and not in the land. They constitute the *real estate* of the South. They are the basis of southern wealth, and therefore it is, that those States look to them with attention, care, and jealousy.

This domestic relationship of master and servant, is called slavery, and when this word slavery passes the slave States, it shocks the nerves of the ignorant bigot or fanatic; for being ignorant of the true relation, he associates with the word *slavery*, all the horrors of accumulated evils, and forthwith concludes that it is his duty to apply a remedy.

Many said Jinn was a broken old man who had taken up with young Cypress to suck out whatever virility he could muster. But such mannish cares had never really mattered to Jinn, and Cypress knew the real reason he was drawn back to her was the acre where the seed barn sat—or at least what was left of it.

The only home Jinn had ever known. He'd especially needed it that last time after selling himself back to Master Planter, when Master had died and left him free to wander once again. She'd sensed he would be back again soon after that.

So it was on that sultry afternoon when he quit oystering for going on the tenth time and the foreman told him no more flatbottom that Jinn wandered up and down the salt river run alongside the salt marsh looking for something, not really knowing what. Remembering, mostly. But that was when he came upon it.

There it grew—thriving solo—that twelve-branched splendor of flowering cotton glory.

It was not yet August, so the petals still shut were not dirtied by the cross-pollen from the inbred strains nearby in forgotten fields.

If there was love yet to be had in this life, there it was, growing straight up in a humped-up river-edge piece of salt-marsh muck that he would eat if he could, because it looked so damn good.

The sheer sight of it brought Jinn closer to a smile than would ever cross his face in this life, and he stomped the water and marshy loam like an inebriated old drunk until it spattered him up and down, front and back, as if he had laid down in it and slithered along like a north marsh gator.

There was only one place for him now, and so he hand-scooped the silty clay bed around it, carefully exposing no roots and cradling the plant in his muslin pack, having first dumped all other contents into the river.

Jinn needed nothing else now. In that moment, this wilt-free plant might just have saved him, and one last time, he headed home to Cypress.

Stay put.

∅

Many said when weevil brought the destruction, it was a great plague.

They were all being punished again for some inherent evil never really understood.

A chance came, and a chance was taken away by an ugly blight upon the land.

Martha tried to tell her brothers that Teacher shared the specimen, the malice captured in a bottle viewed from household to household.

Even brought it to church, the praise house.

Turn the crop, Teacher pleaded with her former pupils, armed with leaflets from the agricultural inland already swept by its destruction.

Rotate.

Truman and Simon would not listen until the annual thousand-bale yield of Sea Island Cotton dwindled to a hundred the following year.

Then they all knew it was true; if only they had listened.

Cotton would never save them.

∅

Martha was the only Planter family member present when Cypress passed.

She was all that was necessary, really, was what Cypress said.

Master, Salome, Jinn, Kenneth, and the boys were long gone by then, and only the women had since resided at home on the carved-out parcel of old Tabby Place, like sisters guarding an older time.

In wait for what was to come, as eventually it *was* to come.

There would be no peace for them that would last longer than a half-decade. Tribulations were part of existence, and one must be prepared and ready at all times.

Never rest for the weary, the guarded—aged them before their time.

Not so much the work of their daily existence as the waiting on the next pestilence that kept them tired and worn.

Weary.

So it was Martha alone who kept her mother cooled and comforted in the front of the house so she could peer out the east window to Salome's acres and whisper final orders to daughter the same way Cypress had seen Salome out to the great gates to depart a life never chosen or volunteered for.

Both women brought into an existence that had mattered little, yet Martha assumed a purpose and meaning would come from her mother's final words.

Martha needn't have prayed for some sort of an answer, as one came freely in Cypress's whisper, uttered the same time as a pain-shedding breath.

"Keep the land in the family. However you must."

Stay put.

Hold on.

∅

Jinn was long gone by the time Cypress held her ground—literally—against the white hoods.

Their stealth would not dissuade her. In spite of the child hidden away in the house, too scared to look above the quilts, Cypress leveled a two-barrel at the figures who appeared in silhouette behind the stacked-pylon fire.

"Don't belong here!"

Out. Move out.

Or burn you out.

Their taunts failed to pierce her tabby rock-hard pride, and she shot out into the night toward the ocean, a scattered spread of pellets asked and answered only by pounding breakers.

Chicken grit cowards!

She yelled back at those who had floated in through the marsh ways in a game of islander intimidation common in those days, for a landmass owned by the sons and daughters of freedmen may as well have been deserted, and no one much cared anyhow.

Perhaps it was some force of sheer female fortitude that scared them off that night, for this was a fraternity of Confederate grandsons not scared so easily and called to purify the places of anyone perceived to be at the same level as dirt.

Such events did not happen so often anymore; they were pretty much left alone in the long while after the Blues departed.

Tenants for life.

That's what Cypress had told Martha, Truman, and Simon that night, after she'd scared off the hoods and sent them shaking back to bed.

Tenants for life.

No one scaring us out now. Same thing Salome told Cypress that night when Master Planter and Junior let them be.

Hang on. Stay put.

∅

When Missus Planter found the thinly-veiled poem in Master Planter's papers, there was no doubt as to what or who it was truly about.

Silly old fool.

Such nonsense.

She clucked at the weakness of her husband made visible by these words. How inane he had become since the secession talk had begun, as if he held the pen of Rhett or Meminger or even Hammond, who had called out cotton as king among all.

She laughed out her mockery and bitterly placed it back as if undisturbed where she had found it amid old chattel bills of sale and cotton exchange tickets.

Senile hypocrite!

Ode to the Cotton Plant
by Ephraim Planter

Your beauty at dawn parallels the singular lines and rows at dusk
when shadows cloak until the moon casts light into the furrows
over the viewer and the viewed

A symbol of life and future and long lives of family
that deserve the world
Kings and their queens and servants alive or dead
the same as blood
and take hold of all as their own.

My cultivar is in you and I reach each new day
for that light I see through you
my beloved

∅

Jinn was watching out the wide crevice in the seed barn wall that day when Master Planter and Junior turned away from Salome's door.

Turned away.

He grabbed his freedman certificate and hobbled toward the pair walking down the shelled path toward the carriage that had brought them back to this forsaken plantation they used to call home. He hobbled on his cramped legs that had been under him while he peered through a crevice near the floor and had watched aghast as they left Salome and Cypress alone.

Once the sleep left his legs, he ran faster and around the pair and dropped to his knees so quickly they stopped fast in their path, looking down at this man in their way. This man that they'd known so well. Older now. Less broken somehow than he had been at the seed table, but then he peered up at Master with those same eyes, and Master Planter felt that twinge of the old days, as if he were still the lord.

"Get up, Jinn," Junior ordered.

"Out of the way," he demanded.

Jinn began to stand upright and looked Master square in his face.

Master, was all Jinn said as he handed over his freedom on paper to the Master.

"Whatever you think I am worth," he said, handing over liberty longed for, cheered for when the Blues had arrived. Now waved it, desperate.

Confused now as he saw the face of the place he used to reside within, safer somehow then.

Cypress ran out then.

Ran to this man who lived in their seed barn, talked to her, told her stories of the old glory.

Cotton seeds found and lost.

Cotton as beauty. Cotton as life.

Come now, Jinn.

Cypress took his hand.

Salome looked out beyond the cabin door at this shocking scene, astounded by Jinn's begging for possession.

"Jinn!" Salome snarled sense to the misplaced seed man. Together the woman and girl led him away from Master Planter, who did not reach for the paper, another disgrace for a man begging for place and purpose, a reason.

The certainty of rejection by Master Planter, disregarding Junior, forced Jinn to finally sell out to this notion of freedom and took Cypress back down the path in this unlikely existence to find something worth another day.

"We need you, Jinn," Cypress whispered once out of earshot.

Need you.

∅

Master Planter's wife was an Ephraim, and her sister had married a Seabrook, making their children double cousins, as some would say back then. A double cousin meant little compared with a niece or nephew, as the Planters' children were direct heirs to the Planter-Ephraim-Seabrook line and more cotton acres than one could fathom. That became more apparent after the Seabrooks lost both children to yellow fever and looked on their nieces and nephews as surrogate heirs to the future empire.

Missus Planter's genius had been naming her youngest Mikell Ephraim Seabrook Planter so she could share him with her sister. Mikell was christened with his maternal aunt and uncle as witnesses and was the luckiest islander child alive—so his mother told him till he was almost 17 and died for the Confederacy.

His mother was given the news in the great front hall of the summer home, where she smashed all that the Blues had left her.

His burial consumed her for the rest of her days. She cursed the mausoleum her husband had built on an island that would now hold none of them.

Fool. Idiot.

This was what she had of him now.

Cursed, really.

They were all rotted out now in dirt meant for him.

Who knows what a woman who lost her son would do to destroy a man already gutted.

If she could think of it, consider it done.

∅

The Attorney took extra care with the cadence of her words when she informed Martha that Simon's death certificate had been located.

"He called himself Simon Seedman, which had made it more difficult for us to find him. Had you known?"

The Attorney queried a distant Martha about a name when she could only focus on the now-longer list of the dead: Salome, Cypress, Jinn, Kenneth, and Simon.

The waterside cemetery was incomplete. Simon would need to be brought home, as his was a restless spirit that would most certainly wander till it came home.

Martha searched her mind to find where she had been in late 1949. More than twenty years in the ground, and Simon had not been breathing all this time. She'd never even felt his soul depart earth. Never had one visitation.

Truman reached for her hand to bring her back to the present. He felt it too but remained solid for what was next.

"Our father's name," Martha said quietly.

"It was our father's name," Martha said again, claiming a man she had never really called father, only Jinn.

The Attorney nodded as if she did not know this family lineage better than most, honoring the information carried by this woman who held its bits together lest they be scattered beyond her. Lost.

"In some ways, we are all more Seedmans than Planters," Martha said, a tardy response to a question decades long, acres wide, and oceans deep. "Hope Simon finally found his peace, and left it there to find him wherever his body now rested."

They would need to come back tomorrow, as today was now a day for grief, and there was family to tell, which really meant neighbors. Truman shrugged, although he well knew the Attorney understood they would need to go for now.

*Handbook of an Exhibition Illustrating
British Cotton Cultivation
& the Commercial Uses of Cotton*

*Held at the Imperial Institute in Conjunction with the British Cotton
Growing Association.*
Great Britain Commonwealth Institute, 1905

SEA ISLAND COTTON *(Gossypium barbadense, L.)* —
This plant is native to the West Indies, and the name
barbadense indicates its connection with Barbados. The
species was introduced in the United States of America
from the West Indies, and successfully cultivated in the
Sea Islands and neighbouring districts of the Southern States, with the results that its produce is generally
known in commerce as "Sea Island Cotton."

The seeds are covered with long, fine, silky hairs,
the lint, without any admixture of the short hairs, or
linters, characteristic of Upland Cotton see (*G. hirsu-
tum*). The length of the staple varies from $1^{3/8}$ to $2^{1/2}$
inches, and its length, together with its fine silky nature, renders Sea Island the most valuable of all cottons.

∅

For the Developer, island land was a great blank canvas on which to create with divine inspiration. For the supreme planters of Sea Island Cotton, it was sustenance of divine inspiration. For Cypress, it was more than lofty imaginings.

A seed propagates a life.

It is life that needs land to survive as much as seed needs its soil.

It is the land that transcends.

Dirt. Marsh mud.

But no one could own the sea, and the land was what it was because of the sea.

Land cannot be bound by paper alone, cannot be confined fully any more than one man can possess another's soul.

Yet too many on this island had tried.

Martha kicked off the rocks of Jinn's unmarked plot that day at the water's-edge cemetery. It was closest to Cypress, just to the right, so Martha had always assumed it was Jinn who lay there. *Had to be*, she said as Truman watched.

Spacing felt right when she reached for the childhood memory as she knelt before all of them this time.

Had her brothers not made her so chin-hard angry when they'd run off and she'd remained in this godforsaken place to live out all their mother had taught them.

Perhaps it was Martha who had needed saving after all. Maybe staying put was her running. No matter now that she was not alone.

Now it was for all of them again.

Stay put. Hold on.

∅

Many said Sea Island Cotton was the fabric of royalty.

Yet cotton was the only king ever to reign on the island, in spite of Master Planter's grandiosity and faux benevolence.

In spite of his desire to be Lord.

Like many a despot before him, he had loved what was his alone and never shared.

His land.

His cotton.

His children. His wife.

His chattel.

In that precise order.

Mostly, he had loved his seed. Or what he thought had been his alone.

In the end, what was given had been taken.

Ol Conjur had surely warned him, but he had failed to listen back then.

Amazing how open a man's ears become when close to the dirt.

∅

The Developer loved the island.

He loved its isolation, its desolation, and its sheer potential.

The only problem was its inhabitants.

The islanders would be ousted soon enough, he had convinced himself, but still he feared them as you would a child starved for attention, gently pushing him or her away as if to say quietly:

Enough now.

Never quite understanding what was needed or desired, the need to be loved was such a deterrent when it came as a demand. This was how he viewed the islanders.

Needy. Desperate, really.

Too peculiar, he thought, and much too unpredictable for his liking, they were, so they must simply be put out. He had no desire to deal with them directly, so he sent his people.

His advisors. His lawyers. *Take care of them.*

He need not engage his disgust with those he perceived as less than he. Though their acres outnumbered his at present ten to one, that ratio would turn soon enough, he had no doubt.

He just wanted to get on with it, and he told them so.

Get him the island.

So to work they went.

Sea Island Plantation, he would call it.

What a plantation should be: a new kingdom rising out of this half-bogged dirt.

No one since Master Planter had seen what lay within this soil like the Developer did.

He raised images of Scottish golf, pleasing him as he swung an imaginary club pointed east, and savored thoughts of hushed crowds lining a course whipped along by unpredictable oceanside breezes and deep-wet bunkers.

Strategically bungalow-lined fairways and a singular flag hovering just beyond the island center at water's edge on top of this old plantation site that was now all his.

Almost all.

He had convinced his father's timber partners that the forests and wildlife should be preserved and hidden among what would emerge as the most private and exclusive resort imaginable.

Nature's protector. Clear covenants.

No one had quite brought them together like this; he would be the first.

It was only in those fraught early morning hours the other voices ever really haunted him.

That first dig at about a hundred yards from what would be the eighteenth pin was where they had brought up the first skull.

Shit. Old graveyard.

That was about all the Developer would mutter that day, and then a more quiet but undoubtedly direct order:

Keep digging.

The Golfer had beamed in that first links classic, unaware he had strutted for tartan plaid and trophy down an emerald green fairway over unnamed field hands who had labored for that first glory of old Tabby Place.

The Developer smiled and finally breathed deep and long: he'd built it, and they had come. Now the island would have a second chance: the twentieth-century plantation.

The Developer and the Golfer smiled in tandem at reporters and television cameras.

A new South.

He had never been more certain of anything.

∅

Jinn had come up from this half-bogged dirt.

In many ways, he'd loved it more than his own life, so putting him back up-to-elbows in it did not bother Cypress as much as it did watching her children experience this passage.

Yes, Jinn had thrived in dirt most certainly.

He had found his purpose in it, the wretched existence only he alone could have survived. It was mainly after the Blues had departed that it was so difficult to determine his place or if he even still had one.

Such a quirk of fate to be handed his free papers and then wander lost for years without Master Planter as his compass, his lead.

Sadly, Jinn had had no idea of the gifts that lay within himself, only uncovered when his hands were up to wrists in this sodden soil, caked with marsh mud. He'd even licked it off himself sometimes, the island mud that had made him a man, given him a place in the world.

Purpose.

As he returned to the underneath side of this sodden Lowcountry soil he loved so much, he once again became a part of it, and for that, Cypress was only glad. She cracked the seed barn items he had last touched and placed them near the imperfect cross stuck at the eastern point of the rectangular dig, the old way that Salome had taught her, to settle his restless spirit lest he lead someone else to death's door.

"His soul is now between him and his Lord, his only master now." The praise house deacon let the final words slide into an almost-whisper as Cypress picked up a handful of soggy dirt, looked out over the ocean's skyline as if still in prayer, and dropped it into the shallow grave. She took a long stride backward and watched as her children took a step forward and followed her duty.

This was their father, but a father, he'd never known how to be.

A seed boy turned seed man.

That was what he was, and he'd done his best to be content amid the affliction and the afterward and all the in-between. Of course, he had been blessed to find such contentment in seed and fodder when so many others never knew none of it, before or after.

Jinn had had no answers for anybody. Certainly no lessons for these children.

"We respect the dead," Cypress ordered her children, as if speaking for Jinn's regret now that he could not. Not that he ever would have spoken of it living and breathing.

There were very few days in her life that Cypress had cried, but the day she buried Jinn was to be one of them, so much so that she fell into a crumpled heap when they turned to walk the narrow paths back to home. She fell to her knees in front of her children, something her former staid self would never have done, and she sobbed and sobbed, not for the man so much as the theft of his life and purpose by another.

And simply because a new death brings sadness for past deaths and the ultimate finality of it all.

She cried for the chances lost Jinn would never grieve for and could not take back for himself—in life or death.

It was then when she put her hands on her thighs to push herself back up from that sodden dirt that she saw it.

"Get me the trowel!" she yelled at Truman, who was still frozen from watching his mother in such a state.

"Get me my trowel!" she screamed again, and Simon lit off in a dead run.

There was no mistaking the one singular plant in a crop of wilt standing in a straight-up salute in honor of all that Jinn had lost and all that was yet to be gained for his children.

Its yellow flower a gift no doubt from Salome or Jinn or whomever lay beneath this scrap back-forty acre of old Tabby Place near the graveyard. It had been the one place that even Master Planter had let them gather in peace to bury their own near the water's edge. A space used to lay their dead since the days the Captain had owned this land.

It may as well have been delivered via messenger on the Missus' silver platter, as there was no doubting this wilted plant held a crystal-clear call to carry on.

Cypress didn't need ol Conjur to tell her this now. It was a tone she heard high and loud and lucid as if a silver bell had rung above the crane overhead that now swooped her in that moment on her knees in the half-bogged dirt, tears melting dirt as she swiped her face to witness the return before her.

"I see you, Jinn."

See you.

Cypress whispered to this tall, straight, proud Carolina Sea Island Cotton plant nestled among the wilt, thriving here on some back acre no longer curated by whipped field hands who hovered over children lest they take a lash in their stead all for the sake of pounds per acre.

"Free now," she whispered again

See you.

She could barely offer the real goodbye to the friend she had held as she'd watched his eyes whither like the wilt and foulness and black-arm that had attacked this back parcel of old Tabby Place. No one wanted this acre of failed cotton eaten 'live by covetous demons that had excavated planters from their homes—except, of course, the developers to come, those ravenous sharks who would push her daughter like no other test she would pass save her life.

There would be no more crying for Cypress after the day she buried Jinn and watched his soul return in spirit as a cotton plant to tell her there was more.

Much more.

∅

"Praise house," Martha directed when she and Truman returned to the car the day they learned of their lost brother.

"Then we need to find Jolene," Martha ordered, and Truman pretended to agree. "All we have left of Simon now."

Need to bring her in tight.

∅

The land promises of the Blues never really changed Salome or even Jinn for that matter; he preferred sifting through seeds to letting crumbled soil slip through his fingers as the next generation did as they grieved that last lost cotton crop.

Cypress had watched both sets of folks suffer in the dirt for the sake of the long-lint. Watched it scoop up the conceit and guff of men who might otherwise have been haughty and sure.

Puffed up.

In Salome's day, permission to set a man or woman's will free after augured punishment was rarely enforced, threatened, by a seer's glint eye or glance, as if one had already been inflicted.

Forever would they watch for that glance.

That intended backhand. Fend off a slight before it ever landed. They had learned to look down, kept down in arms, legs, and spirit alike. Shackles were not needed once words and sheer menace became a captor's best arsenal.

A simple promise of land was more than a gift of providence: it was deserved.

Only fitting. A redemption.

It was what the Blue General had ordered.

Give them land, and all will be healed.

Self-sufficient.

Freed.

∅

Simon would have been pleased by the way they had cordoned off his body as if it were some important Harlem crime scene when in fact he had simply and finally had a moment where he'd imbibed more juice and junk than his poor body would allow.

Thanks to weevil.

His friends knew Simon had blamed it all on weevil, as he'd openly and widely reported gratitude toward the homely beetle for getting him out.

Out and away from a South he'd detested more than his mother.

He'd never looked back.

Sea Island cotton had been on its way out, and he'd tried oystering and seasonal gigs in Savannah and even Charleston, but none of it had stuck—or he'd never stuck to it, as Cypress would say—and he'd joined a band of minstrels leaving from the juke joint one night with some other brothers and sisters from different mothers and headed with them to Harlem.

At Lenox and Seventh, he had found a new place where he'd fit, mostly, and had hung there till Helena had found him and tried to own him, sounding just a bit too much like she had a Cypress tongue, and he'd steered clear of her. She'd stuck around long enough to be carrying Jolene but had decided to head back to her mama in Weeksville and not let this baby be born among people she hardly knew.

Or who really cared to try anymore, for that matter.

Oh, but Simon had known them. In fact, he'd known nearly all of them. If not them, he'd known their mama or grandpap or niece or cousin or baby bro and aunt sis. Every last one of them had come from the island to settle in concrete dank like him, fed up with failed fibers and unfed desire.

Run north.

On this corner, he'd known every street crooner and banjo man and sun-guarded hussy draping the streets at dawn.

He'd syncopated the moments between dusk and sunrise and called it 'my bang,' like he alone had owned the night and the street it settled on.

In some ways, he truly had, and it had only been when Simon had realized these brothers and sisters would pay for just about anything to escape their too-long day-to-day that money had begun rolling in and he'd begun rolling it up. Simon had finally found his need.

Up and up and up.

High was never enough for Simon.

More had no top.

Bottom was a new day climb.

Those mornings, Simon felt low as the scum on a flat-bottom marsh slider, the kind of gunk that would embed and never come off, stuck on for dear life to a South in his bones that crept in at the strangest moments. He could forget all that in a pure urban haze of jazz and solid laughin' and screamin' till four a.m. or until he'd passed out, and most nights, it had been the latter.

Yes, Simon had owned the night and was eventually owned by it.

Same Jinn's shadows, really, but different here somehow.

His time.

His weak spot.

A need, really.

Cypress always said if a man actually found what he loved, he should work it.

Live it. Breathe it.

So that's what he'd done—*make mama proud.* He'd laughed off the shakes as he reached for his peaks till they killed him one night in a cold, dark room on the second floor of that row house as far north of the island as he could have run.

Cordoned off.

Never see his baby girl now. They'd look in and said it gently amongst themselves.

Simon had finally run up and run out.

∅

Some were beckoned. Some were driven.

Men Truman had known his entire life were determined to leave the island in a post-cotton disarray.

What to do. What to do.

The open gates to European immigrants had long since closed, and the industrial North needed them as laborers. At last they were necessary.

Again.

It was that deeply-rooted need to be essential—to have a place—a call that rapped so strongly and tugged even more tightly at their desires.

Not all about the cost of food. A need.

Even deeper.

Kenneth was drunk most times now, and Martha somehow believed she could hold it all together on her own, which left such a bad taste in Truman's mouth that he could no longer listen.

It was time for something better, and he had decided something better beckoned north.

Truman had met with the agent twice, and those blue-sky promises of work and dollar-per-hour were laughable, but even if the agent was only half-right, he was more than interested.

Each night as he lay down for shuteye, Truman saw the future.

It was his. Clean.

Vivid. Touchable.

By the time Truman arrived in Chicago, the urban league worked to greet every single Southern laborer to ensure they were known, brought in close and tight—had a place here among others.

It would never be the South, and for that, Truman was not alone in a head-to-toe ejection of cathartic relief.

No cotton-picking here.

Got that right. No one would go near a mill.

The cold hard steel of bolt cutting would replace all that lint.

Done with it.

The hard, fast work consumed Truman for those first years, and he was indispensable within something larger, faster, more challenging than any other work he had ever done. No more dirt.

It fed him. Kept him alive.
His true north. Forget the South.

∅

Martha took to her grave exactly what she told Jolene the day she finally found her. Met with her. Brought her in tight.

Many were left to ponder for years to come what exactly was exchanged between these daughters of Cypress. Martha owned that final hold-on once she shared it with kin. She had begun with just enough tale, a story deeper and wider than anywhere else ever told.

Land has a soul.

Others imagined Martha began with the story of her grandmother's shackles, a Blue invasion, a child born free, a native son's struggle to exist within this land-soul-purpose, lost in tired means of making it.

Martha condensed a child's lessons into those few hours, lessons she'd been offered year after year until they'd taken, and touched Simon within his child until she could hear those words and knew them to resonate strong and true.

For a truth can be released only once it is felt in the bones, ol Conjur would have said. *It will rise up till you shout it, unleash it,* Cypress would have said.

Released from the bones of the sacred spirits of those who'd lacked choice and those who'd given all for the future in spite of that lack. It was a privilege to carry on for them.

A hallowed privilege.

In spite of a clouded title, the answers were clear that afternoon, and Martha reached into Jolene somehow to fix in her the clarity of a wisdom that only comes through upbringing.

Released. Unleashed.

Jolene ran back north then with her mother in tow and never looked back. *It was not her place to remain here,* she declared as she rushed out the door early the next morning. Barely goodbye. Yet long enough to make the stop at the Attorney's office and sign the necessary in spite of her mother's hissing to relinquish her share in a property that was much more than dollars or dirt.

Land has a soul, she hushed her mama, and Martha respectfully kept her mouth corners in place.

Gave Martha clear title. The Attorney slapped her hand on the desk and laughed hearty.

No one was more shocked than Truman.

It was over, and Martha could then smile as if she already knew.

Ø

When news of Simon circled the island, everyone visualized Martha's reaction.

Many had begun to understand a man's need to rid himself of this life here amid a higher and lower sense of self.

No matter how hard one strived, it seemed it all could be lost in an instant.

A lifetime of loss. And now more loss still.

Most knew full well why the boys had run north, taking different routes, with no desire to return.

Crossed their minds, too, if they could only admit it aloud.

∅

Salome had been the first to die intestate but not without title.

As a free woman, she had hung on to her plot of old Tabby Place till her last breath.

Held on through the amnesty and repurchase. One heir. Land passed on mother to daughter like in the old ways.

Salome was the ancestor, and all the rest to come after were heirs to the property record that the Attorney came to believe might be her own unraveling or purpose. Wasn't sure which. So she'd rolled up her sleeves at that first event, when as a young law clerk she had heard the Reverend's message.

Heard the calling, and there was no looking back now.

Opportunity. Use it for good.

Change the world. For right. For good.

She had even helped with the language of that second proclamation, and now almost a decade had passed and the Reverend was dead, but the work remained.

And the work here suited her.

The day the Reverend was shot, she heard the news on the island and crumpled with those she was meant to prop up. Yet she knew then there was no leaving this work now.

Too much to do. *Must be done.*

The Attorney would remain on the island, as done was a day not likely coming anytime soon.

Back home was not a place she wanted to be, with her insular family who never saw the gray on their black-and-white RCAs. Six o'clock, dinner and the evening news worlds away.

Comfortable. Secure.

This was necessary. Uncomfortable. All the rest mattered little, though, as she touched Salome Planter's title. It was the first she had seen in existence, and even touching the faded paper felt right and good.

Clear and necessary.

In the end, it would teach her all she needed to know about reasons to stay.

Hold on. See it through.

∅

So it would be on the Tuesday after the Developer's failed partition attempt that Martha would finally lift up the worn-in linoleum crevice off-center in the step-up kitchen floor and remove that flat, heavy-lead box filled with tattered-edge documents. She cautiously picked out the ledger record stamped *1870 Census* as meticulously as a faithful Southern civil servant who likely winced in unaffected pain over such post-war truths.

August 5, 1870
Location: Sea Island Parish, South Carolina
Head of household: Salome Planter
24 years
Female (former slave)
Unmarried
(B) Black
Place of birth: ~~*N'gula*~~ *S.C.*
Occupation—Farming
Attended school—Blank
Cannot Read—Checked; Cannot Write - Checked
Value of Real Estate—48 acres valued at $480 (40 tillable)
Value of Personal Estate—Blank
Cypress Planter, daughter, 8 years, M (Mulatto)
Attended school—Checked; Cannot Read—Blank; Cannot Write— Checked

Gives me strength when I see this.
Box in her lap, Martha spoke preacher-like to Jolene. She held the record up in her flat, colorless palm to a stooped-over Jolene, who was still trying to read over her shoulder.
Land rich and cash poor.
If she could hold on then, we must now.

∅

Jolene was not her father's daughter that day but her grandmother's, Martha would say later. *Girl finally knew her own mind.*

Perhaps it had not been Martha's persuasion after all but some deep, dark night visitation from Cypress the night before. Truman wished he could have seen his mother's specter himself, along with those truths she'd spewed like no other. In the moment of triumph, it came through as if a prayer for General relief. Cypress spoke to his heart.

Land is us, my dear son.

You and me. Connected.

Land gives not just a place for home but the answer to who we are inside.

Our souls.

Our hearts.

Lives in your mind.

It persists when we cannot.

It returns to us when we think we have nothing left to give.

Strength. Purpose.

Never fails us.

Always is, always was here.

In turn, it only asks us for one thing.

Care. Always fragile and new.

Jolene woke that next morning spurred to run off the island as fast and far north as she could, back to her own familiar. To find her own truth. She shook her startled mother and packed up in haste, something like Missus Planter had done before the Blues arrived.

Not run away. Run toward.

The last Martha heard from Jolene's mother's people was that Jolene had not followed her back to Weeksville but veered off instead for Detroit. She now placed curls that framed faces of backup singers and lived off a new sound.

Found her tune at last, they said all the way back in Harlem.

After all, Simon's daughter.

∅

Resort developers multiplied in the eighties and nineties, and by the new millennium, the island was a regular on the cover of *Oceanscapes* and *Coastal Traveler* and numerous other resort-escape magazines drooled over in doctors' waiting rooms up north.

Luxurious. Elite. Blue water views.

It took well into another century before the coastal corridor found any protection from congress, and possessory heirs who had no intention of leaving felt a temporary reprieve from the constant badgering.

Yet the property tax was another matter for some, and many an heir held fast but lost the economic fight when a new resort went up next door along with the tax bill.

Forfeiture then became the new game of chance, as developers waited like vultures for sheriff's sales on the courthouse steps. Bartering still to squander freedmen's legacies for miniature golf, bicycle paths, and a poolside chaise lounge.

Wagers over plots grew between speculators like the old plantation traders who'd fed on gossip and insider news from the loudest mouths who never bit their tongue when ignited by emotion and inequity like a bad card hand.

Still others hold on.

Heirs reside on twenty- or forty-acre tracts still titled in the name of the singular freed man or woman from when the midnight read of a proclamation brought chaos like no one had ever seen.

Stay put.

Hold on.

∅

The lone surviving cypress tree was protected within an island preserve that neighbored Salome's parcel. *It was all the Developer ever did for old Tabby Place besides lining his pockets,* former neighbors—losers of their own partition battles—had said with the bitterness of old salt marsh in their mouths. Even though most of the acres had clear titles back to Master Planter's grandfathers, indigo, and rice, so few were able to hold their ground.

Parcels were sold out by non-possessory heirs who'd had enough of the cotton aftermath for very different reasons.

When it came to the island, there was no real clear winner following the Blue invasion. Loss was really the only constant for many. The tree that had brought life to so many now had many more than three knees surrounding it, like multiple litters of heirs that exponentially distributed themselves among the wet land, the beach, beyond.

Some close, others far. Some very far.

Yet it remained stalwart, ancestral.

The origin that gave life to others kept its center, kept its corner of earth needed for sustenance and future.

Stay put. Hold on.

Unfortunately, the island corridor was not as secure as the old tree, and parcel after parcel was later tugged, ripped, or lost due to those cloudy titles. Locals read the latest partition sale postings in Beaufort in the *Island News* classifieds, calling for heirs to come forward.

Name themselves.

Most knew full well there would always be at least one who chose cash over land. Cash over family. *Take care of our own.*

Older ones just shook their heads, for they knew the youngers did not remember.

∅

A newer prefab home rests by a faded pulp sign tacked to its tilted, half-uprooted post on the corner where Blackgum Tree Road intersects with the highway that pumps tourists by the second onto the island this time of year.

Freetown.

One can still make out if they read closely. Take the time to see.

Or even more time to listen closely, hear the rattletrap sharp staccato of ol Granny in the kitchen house or the broken-up wail of Cypress wrestled up from the water's edge in overlapped whispers. Overlain in years. Overlain by choice.

Always just one good reason to hold on.

Just one good reason.

Stay put.

AFTERWORD

The particular strain of Sea Island Cotton raised in the Lowcountry was both a blessing and a curse for more than Salome's heirs. It brought wealth and riches to an imperial lineage of Sea Island families and one of the cruelest and most inhumane acts of evil conspired since the Roman Empire. Yet something so precious can slip away as easily as it arrives, and those who once possessed it more than reaped what they had sown. Optimists tried to revive Master Planter's seeds more inland, in places like Georgia and Florida, but interior Sea Island Cotton never found the same glory. Of course, the interiors never had Jinn or ol Conjur or Salome or Cypress, or even Martha, for that matter. The bales at the Cotton Exchange were never again stamped with *Planter*, which had always brought the highest price and had tricked all the other planters into false self-importance, giving them the impression that it was *them* who had created the magnificent long-staple that thrived alongside the mosquito and reaped off the shredded, weathered fingertips of those denied personhood. Yet even now, there are always those who see money as more than paper, who forget the very source from whence it comes, and instead employ bondage and servitude out of fear and voracity to keep clutching, grasping, strangling, and drowning in all the pulp-driven soul-trappings of this material life. How very odd that those lingering seeds of Master Planter's strain were left in a drawer at the USDA inland office after the interior crop failed, and no one has seen them hence. Sure, the genetic base can be found in cotton strains across the world today, but those will never ever come close to Master Planter's Lowcountry Sea Island Cotton. Assuredly, ol Conjur would proffer the imagining that there may still be that one lone long-staple hand-selected by Jinn hidden away in that drawer's crevice or seam, a seed holding the remarkable genetic line of a single cotton strain, its planters, and all their heirs, free or otherwise. That lifetime of bondage for so many before them confined within one seed to be released from what imprisoned them when Martha somehow mustered the old grit and held fast to what Salome and Cypress had preached, and at long last, they broke through. One day, someone may find that solitary seed tucked away in a wooden drawer cranny, plant it, cultivate, and grow once again the most beautiful long fiber ever to clothe a deity.

In Gratitude

While a work of historical fiction takes many liberties, this one is factually grounded thanks to many who have worked much more diligently than I to protect the historical record of the challenges and inequities regarding Lowcountry heirs' property. I am indebted to the Southern Historical Collection: Louis Round Wilson Special Collections Library, UNC-Chapel Hill, where I was a visiting researcher supported by Northcentral University. I am thankful to those whose vigilance continues to protect the record of this passage, including Dr. Emory Campbell and his enduring and poignant voice of Gullah culture and protection of heirs' property rights; the volunteers at The Hilton Head Heritage Library; The Penn Center, St. Helena Island; the Edisto Island Historic Preservation Society and Museum, and especially the Charles Spencer collection of Edisto history; attorney and scholar Faith Rivers James; Auburn University researchers Janice F. Dyer and Conner Bailey; Charles Jarrett of Ohio Southern University; Richard Dwight Porcher and Sarah Fick, authors of *The Story of Sea Island Cotton,* a weighty tome I first saw on that Penn Center bookstore shelf and inspired many aspects of this story; plus Dominique T. Hazzard, for her stirring Wellesley honors thesis: *The Gullah People, Justice, and the Land on Hilton Head Island: A Historical Perspective*, a best monograph of these inequities. Also, so grateful to *Crab Fat Magazine* and *Trampset* for first publishing the Prologue and Simon's end story as flash fiction, and to Carol Wise and Sarah Kettle for their immaculate editing. Mostly to my daughter, son-in-law, and husband for putting up with it all.

OTHER ANAPHORA LITERARY PRESS TITLES

The History of British and American Author-Publishers
By: Anna Faktorovich

Notes for Further Research
By: Molly Kirschner

The Encyclopedic Philosophy of Michel Serres
By: Keith Moser

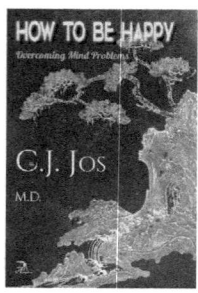

The Visit
By: Michael G. Casey

How to Be Happy
By: C. J. Jos

A Dying Breed
By: Scott Duff

Love in the Cretaceous
By: Howard W. Robertson

The Second of Seven
By: Jeremie Guy

CPSIA information can be obtained
at www.ICGtesting.com
Printed in the USA
BVHW010316050219
539434BV00006BA/84/P